That Fernhill Summer

By Colby Rodowsky

That FERNHILL SUMMER

Colby Rodowsky

FARRAR STRAUS GIROUX / NEW YORK

www.fsgkidsbooks.com

Library of Congress Cataloging-in-Publication Data
Rodowsky, Colby F.
    That Fernhill summer / Colby Rodowsky.— 1st ed.
        p.   cm.
    Summary: Having grown up knowing nothing about her artist mother's estranged family,
thirteen-year-old Kiara spends the summer getting acquainted with her cousins and trying
to understand her complex and cranky grandmother.
    ISBN-13: 978-0-374-37442-6
    ISBN-10: 0-374-37442-2
    [1. Grandmothers—Fiction.   2. Family—Fiction.   3. Interpersonal relations—Fiction.
4. Artists—Fiction.   5. Racially mixed people—Fiction.]   I. Title.

PZ7.R6185Tha 2006
[Fic]—dc22

                                                                                2005047715

For Larry

That Fernhill Summer

1

I didn't know I had an Aunt Claire until the phone rang one Tuesday in June. The day, up to that point, had been strictly garden-variety. In the morning I'd gone to basket-ball practice at the Y and then eaten lunch at my friend Pilar's, and from the moment I got home at two-thirty, I'd had my nose stuck in *A Tree Grows in Brooklyn*. Which I was hurrying to fin-ish so I could go back to the beginning and start again.

The call came just before five o'clock, and there wasn't any-thing about the ring as it echoed through our New York City apartment that said *special*. Just an ordinary ring, on an ordinary Tuesday. But I ran for it anyway, scooping up the receiver just before the machine clicked on, because if there's one thing I hate, it's trying to talk over the message.

"Hello," I said.

"Joyce?" The woman's voice was husky and sort of abrupt.

"No, this is Kiara."

"Joyce's daughter?"

"Yes," I said, wishing whoever this was would get off the phone so I could go back to Francie Nolan and her infinitely more interesting life.

"This is your Aunt Claire, and I'd like to speak to your mother."

I squeezed the book in my right hand until the finger marking my place turned numb. I rammed the phone up against my left ear, as if by grinding it into my head I could make sense of what this woman was saying. I opened my mouth and closed it again.

"My who?" I managed to say after what seemed to be a very long time.

"Your Aunt Claire—your mother's oldest sister. Now, I do need to speak to Joyce," she said, sounding even huskier and more abrupt than she had before.

"She's—my mom, I mean—she's not home. But I could give you her cell phone number."

"I'm not sure that's a good idea," the woman said. "I wouldn't want to catch her at an inopportune time—but I need to get hold of her as soon as possible."

"Well, she only went to the dentist and then afterward she was going to stop at the store and get blueberries." I wondered why I was saying all this, but kept right on babbling. "And maybe even vanilla ice cream to go under the blueberries, if they're nice ones. Anyway, she's probably at the blueberry part by now, or else walking along West End Avenue on her way home. So you could call her."

"What I have to tell her is not good news," the Aunt Claire person said. "It's about your grandmother."

"Granny Bee? In Newark?" My knees wobbled and I reached for a chair. "What's wrong?"

"Your *mother's* mother," she said. "Your grandmother Zenobia. She's very sick. Now, maybe you'd better give me that number. And tell Joyce, in case I don't reach her, that I'll call her back at home as soon as I can."

I gave her the number, said goodbye, and hung up, then sat staring at the bowl of wooden apples on the kitchen table, trying to sort this all out. Because the thing is, I didn't know my mother had a sister, *or* a mother—or an anything else.

Well, actually, I guess I did know, because *everyone* has, or had, a mother—except a clone. And my mother definitely wasn't one of those, otherwise it'd be all over the tabloids every time she did anything. I can just see the headlines: CLONE VACATIONS ON NANTUCKET, CITY CLONE TRAPPED IN ELEVATOR. CLONE AND DAUGHTER ON THE ICE AT ROCKEFELLER CENTER.

My mother is, instead, just my mother. She is Joyce Elizabeth Jones, wife of Warren Birkell, and mother of me, Kiara Jones-Birkell. She is tall (except next to my dad, who is *really* tall), not quite blond, with hair that is long and shiny and smooth to touch. She plays the recorder (but not very well), likes going to the gym, can't pass a bookstore without stopping, would rather eat out than in, and just had her first children's picture book published this past spring. Actually, she'd worked for years at a children's bookstore in the neighborhood and had always prided herself on finding just the right book for each kid.

5

It took a lot of talking, but my dad and I finally persuaded her to quit that job so she can be a full-time illustrator. She calls it trading other people's teddy bears for her own, except her bears have a bit of an attitude, and the book got starred reviews in two magazines and six inches in *The New York Times Book Review*.

Another thing about my mother is that she's always willing to talk to me about anything, at any time. Unless it involves her *family* family (as opposed to her regular family, which is Dad and me). It's as though an invisible fence had been set up around that part of her life. And while our apartment is filled with pictures of generations of Birkells, all looking strangely like my father, and photos of Mom and Dad and me line tabletops and bookcases and windowsills, when it comes to Joneses—there's nothing.

Though there were tons of things I had to be taught *not* to do (like picking my nose or playing with matches), not asking about my mom's family was somehow the one thing I grew up knowing from the start. And I never did, *except* for that one time when I was ten and we'd just come home from Grandpa David and Granny Bee's, and I screwed up my courage and said, "How come we never go to *your* parents' house or see all the people in *your* family?"

My mother turned a spooky greenish-white that day. She curled her lips in till there was nothing left but a thin red line. Her eyes were slits and her hands shook as she said, "Don't ask that, Kiara. Please, don't ask that ever again." And with that, she went into her room and didn't come out until the next morning. Which she has never done before or since.

That night, when Dad and I were eating our favorite snack of graham crackers and milk (graham crackers *in* milk, all mooshed up) at the kitchen table, I tried again. "How come we never see *Mom's* family? How come there's not another set of grandparents or cousins or uncles or aunts? And why did Mom get all upset like that?"

"I can't answer any of that, baby. One, because I don't fully understand, and two, because that's your mother's to deal with. And when she does, then I'm sure she'll tell us."

"But you must know something," I whined. "You must *want* to know."

My father shook his head. "Not a little bit," he said. "Not the least little bit—until *she's* ready." Then he went back to spooning what was left of the graham cracker moosh into his mouth.

That pretty much sums up my father: he's laid back to the point of being totally unflappable. Other significant things to know are that he's a big, bearish sort of a man, with bits of gray around the edges of his dark hair and crinkles in his face that come from laughing a lot. He teaches writing at Columbia University, and is the author of some really terrific books (which get whole pages in *The New York Times Book Review*), and one was even a finalist for a Pulitzer Prize in fiction two years ago. And, he's African American.

Which explains why I am the color of mocha latte with sort of faded hair that looks like a bush, no matter what I do with it. Basically, I'm black and white (but mooshed, like the graham crackers and milk—not striped) with an Irish name that means "little and dark." I like my name, both the way it sounds and how it looks on paper, but especially because my parents' other choice, the one they *didn't* name me, was Unity. I feel that I have been spared.

We live on the Upper West Side of New York City, which is a pretty cool place to live and where lots of people are a bunch of different colors and speak a bunch of different languages. I go to a school four and half blocks away called Rivercrest, which is also cool. The only thing wrong with it is that my teachers are forever asking if I'm going to write, like my father, or draw, like my mother. As if those were the only choices in the whole world. I'm actually trying to decide between being an actress, a veterinarian, or a photographer of exotic places like Tibet or Outer Mongolia.

I think about being an actress because I try out for every play we do at Rivercrest, and just this year I was the White Witch in a musical of Narnia and got to sing these really terrific solos. My Aunt Martha, my dad's sister, said I was a natural. As for the vet part, the only animals I know well are our cat, Gladiator, and Granny Bee's dog, Fred, but I feel I've bonded with both of them. The photography might be more of a stretch, but mostly I fall back on that because I can't think of any other way to get to exotic places. Unless I wait till I'm lots older and go on one of those tours Grandpa David and Granny Bee are always taking.

Anyway, that Tuesday after the phone call, I pushed my chair back and got up, all the while trying to figure what would happen when Aunt Claire got through to Mom as she stood checking out blueberries at the Korean fruit stand. I felt drifty and unattached and wanted to talk to someone, but my father was in Boston speaking at a seminar, and the whole thing seemed much too complicated to explain to any of my friends. Especially since *I* didn't even understand it. I went over to the refrigerator and found my father's itinerary stuck under a tooth-shaped magnet from the dentist's. I ran my finger down the schedule till I got to *Tuesday: 5 p.m.*, where it said *Interview on local radio station.*

"So much for that," I said out loud. I was still standing there, staring at the front of the refrigerator and mindlessly re-arranging the magnets, when I heard the door of our apartment open.

"Mom?" I called.

She didn't answer me, but I heard her coming along the hall to the kitchen. When she got to the doorway, her face was that same spooky greenish-white it had been when I asked the question I wasn't supposed to ask three years ago.

"You have about twenty minutes to throw some clothes in a bag," she said, her voice sounding flat and low. "And then we're going."

2

My mother said to hurry up. She said to use my blue duffel bag and to take shirts and shorts and underwear, and my toothbrush, of course. She said to throw in something halfway decent-looking, like a skirt or maybe the green-and-white dress from the Gap, and somehow I figured this wasn't the time to tell her that that dress made me look like a cucumber every time I wore it.

All that—but she didn't say where we were going.

She called our downstairs neighbor about coming in to feed Gladiator, and left a message on my father's cell phone—but all I could make out was "My sister Claire called, and I have to go. I'll talk to you later."

"Okay, Kiara, you ready? Let's go," Mom said as she sailed past my room, heading for the front door. I picked up my duffel and my straw bag with the word *Jamaica* looped across the front, shoving my wallet and my book down inside it. I stuck in a copy of my mother's picture book, too, because having it made me feel sort of secure. "I'm coming," I said, trailing her down the hall.

"All right," she said, stopping to check the stuff inside her purse the way grownups do. "I've got money, credit cards, my cell phone—are you going like *that*?" My mother looked at me as if I were suddenly sporting a vampire costume, complete with fangs.

"What's wrong with what I have on?" I asked. "It's what I always wear, in summer, anyway." I looked down at my denim shorts and gave my yellow T-shirt a tug. "Besides, everything else is packed."

"In flip-flops? You're going in *flip-flops*?"

"Hey, they're my *best* flip-flops, with the pink flowers on them." I wiggled my toes, then stopped, hoping she wouldn't notice that I'd painted my toenails with her Lavender Dream polish. "Besides—"

"I know," Mom said, "and let me guess—your other shoes are packed. Right? Well, let's go." She hustled me out in front of her, turning to fasten the gazillion locks on the apartment door while I pushed the button for the elevator.

"If Dad has the car in Boston, then how are we going to get wherever it is we're going?" I asked as we got out of the elevator on the ground floor.

"Train," Mom said. "A taxi to the station and then a train." She pushed through the outside door and turned right, heading for Broadway, where it's easiest to find a cab.

When we got to the corner, I dumped my duffel bag on the

sidewalk next to her suitcase and said, "Where *are* we going, then? What *place*?"

"To Baltimore, of course," my mother said, as she lunged into the street to hail a taxi, which kept right on going. As did the next and the next and the one after that. "Baltimore. In Maryland," Mom said, as if I were geographically challenged or something. We waited forever, until finally a cab pulled up to let a man out and Mom almost knocked him down tossing our stuff into the backseat. And that more or less ended it for conversation because once she'd told the driver where we wanted to go Mom scrunched down in the seat and stared at the back of his head, as if she were counting hairs or zits or maybe moles.

There's something about Penn Station that makes you hurry even if you're not *in* a hurry (which apparently we were), and as soon as we were out of the cab Mom took off, looking back over her shoulder from time to time and calling, "Stay with me, Kiara. Stay with me."

We stopped first at the ticket counter and then at the arrivals and departures board before we were off again. "Come on," said Mom, nudging me with her suitcase. "There's a train leaving in ten minutes." And suddenly we were being propelled down the escalator and along the platform and into a car with what seemed like an entire army of other people. We worked our way down the aisle, and about halfway along Mom pushed me into a seat next to a white-haired woman in a pink pantsuit. "You grab this one and I'll find something farther on," she said.

After waiting to make sure my mother found a seat, I hoisted my duffel bag onto the rack overhead and sat down. I didn't even have a chance to get my book out, though, when the woman next to me started in.

"Is that your mother up there in the blue shirt?" she asked, and before I even had a chance to answer, she went on. "And are the two of you off for a vacation? Somewhere fun, I hope."

"Well, yes, I guess. We're going to Baltimore."

"That's lovely, isn't it? You going to visit family there? I always say that visiting family is the best kind of vacation there is. Don't you think so?"

"We visit my grandparents and Aunt Martha in Newark a lot, and my Uncle Charlie and Aunt Mary in Vermont, and once we even went to Montreal to see my Aunt Lily," I said, opening my book and hoping the woman would get the message.

"I've never been to Newark," she went on, "or to Vermont or Montreal, either, though I have been lots of other places. In fact I'm just now on my way home from visiting my grandchildren in Brooklyn." She rummaged in her purse and pulled out a mini photo album with *My Brag Book* printed on the front. "Here they are," she said, leaning toward me, so that I could smell her spicy perfume. "That's Annie—she's seven—and here's Wally, who's ten."

I said "Uuummm" and "Ahhh" at all the right places as she flipped the pages, filling me in on what was happening in every picture. "That's how we grandmothers are," the woman said as she shoved the book back into her bag. "Now, who did you say you were visiting in Baltimore?"

I don't know who I'm visiting in Baltimore. The words shaped themselves in my head, but without even thinking about it, I heard myself say, "My other grandparents. We're visiting my other grandparents."

"Oh, that's fine," she said. "Why, I'll bet they've been running around for days getting ready for your visit. That's what I always do when my grandchildren . . ."

I wanted her to keep quiet so I could think about where we were going and why we were going there and why we'd never been there before. I wanted her to keep quiet so I could think about a grandmother named Zenobia and what was wrong with her, and an Aunt Claire who said she was my mother's *oldest* sister, which meant there had to be another one, and maybe a whole bunch. And mostly I wanted her to keep quiet because I wouldn't know any answers to the questions this woman might ask.

"And what are you going to *do* in Baltimore?" Her voice was like a drill buzzing in my head. "I'll just bet you have wonderful plans."

"Fishing," I said, the word popping up out of nowhere. The way I looked at it, if she wanted a story, then I might as well give her one. "My granddad and I are going fishing. We do it every time I go there and have ever since I was really little. First we dig up worms in the backyard, and then we pack up lunches—peanut butter and jelly sandwiches and lemonade— and then we go *fishing*. And it doesn't matter whether we catch anything or not because when we get home my granny will have made this really outstanding dinner of everything I like. With chocolate cake for dessert." Then I opened my book to page 211 and started to read.

Oddly enough, that seemed to satisfy her, because she took a crossword puzzle out of her bag and settled down to work on it, not saying anything else until we were just on the outskirts of Philadelphia. "This is where I get off," she said, "so why don't you go tell your mother and then she can get my seat before the new people get on." She leaned forward, taking hold of her purse, as if ready to make a dash for it the minute the train came into the station.

I went and got Mom and then settled into the seat by the window, with my mother on the aisle. "Well, you have yourselves a fine vacation," the pantsuit lady said. And then, leaning over Mom so we were almost nose to nose, she added, "And *you* have a fine time fishing with Granddad. And eat a piece of Granny's chocolate cake for me."

"Fishing? With *Granddad*? And *what* Granny's chocolate cake?" my mother said as the train pulled out of Philadelphia. "Where'd *that* come from, Kiara?"

"Well, what was I supposed to say? She kept bugging me, and at first you never bothered to say *where* we're going, and you still haven't said *why*. Anyway, what's the big deal with saying that about grandparents? People do have them, don't they?"

"You don't. My father died five years ago," Mom said, her voice flat and low.

"Five years?" I said. "But five years ago I would've been eight and a half, and I would have known."

"*I* almost had to read about it in the newspaper myself except my sister Claire called very early one morning to say our father had died and there was to be an obituary in *The New York Times* that day. She also said I should pretend that was how I found out he died—from the paper. Claire is terrified of our mother."

"Why?"

"It's a long story, Kiara. Anyway, I waited for the paper to come and then I called my mother on the telephone."

"And?" I prompted.

"She hung up on me. And I didn't go home for the funeral," my mother said.

A cold chill settled over me and I rubbed at my arms to try and get warm. I didn't know what to say. After a long, long time the best I could come up with was, "But why was your father in *The New York Times* when he died?"

"Because he was Lambert Jones, the artist, and he was famous and would never, in a million years, have gone *fishing*. His death was written up in *Newsweek*, too, and *Time*. And they all said he was survived by a wife, two daughters—Claire and Elinor—and four grandchildren." My mother's voice went from flat to pinched.

"And you haven't seen them—any of them?"

"Not for seventeen years."

"And what about the granny and the chocolate cake?" I whispered, almost afraid to ask.

"You have a grandmother named Zenobia who wouldn't know how to make a chocolate cake if that was the only thing between her and starvation. And who would probably gag at the word 'granny.' "

"But she's who the call was about—from the Aunt Claire person, right? What happened to her?"

"She had a fall—she's in the hospital, in a coma—and they don't think she's going to live." And with that my mother seemed to crumple down in her seat even farther.

Neither one of us said anything for a while. We sat listening to the clickety-click of the train, Mom with her eyes closed and me staring out the window. My head was so full of stuff I thought maybe it would explode and splatter all my questions up and down the car.

Seventeen years? How can you not talk to someone for seventeen years? How can you not talk to your mother? Or your father? And why wouldn't you? I thought about Mom and Dad and what it'd be like if they didn't talk to me ever again, and all of a sudden something hurt deep inside of me. *Why? Why?*

"Why?" I said out loud. "Why didn't they talk to you, or you to them?"

"One thing you have to know is that both my mother and father were always very stubborn people," Mom said. "Incredibly stubborn."

"Hah," I snorted. "As if you're not!" That's the thing about *my* mother—she's stubborn as a mule, as a whole bunch or herd or pride of mules. "How about the time you set out to walk from our apartment all the way down to Fourteenth Street, only you had on new shoes that gave you a blister, but you wouldn't catch a bus because you'd said you were going to walk—but then your foot got infected and a couple of days later you had to go to the doctor. How about that?"

"Well, yes," said Mom.

"Or when you said you were going to paint your bedroom green, only by the time you'd done one wall *anybody* could see it was a really putrid shade of green, but you kept right on going—because that's what you'd said you were going to do. And it's *still* a putrid shade of green," I said.

My mother made a funny little noise in her throat that wasn't exactly a yes, or a no, either. Then she reached over and took my hand, locking her fingers in between mine so that it looked as if some monster two-tone ten-finger hand was resting on top of my book.

I stared at that hand, at those two hands, until an idea began to take shape in my head. "Is it because of me? Because of Dad and me? Why your mother didn't talk to you?" I finally asked.

"Maybe—I don't know. I've been back and forth on this for years," she said. "But it wasn't just that. There was always— something else."

"What kind of something else?" I said. "And besides, why didn't you just stop whatever it was?"

"Not now, Kiara," Mom said, sighing. "Not now." And then she pulled her hand away and seemed to go back into that place where she'd been ever since the call came from Aunt Claire.

3

The train station in Baltimore was tons smaller than the one in New York, and instead of running everywhere people were actually *walking*, sometimes taking time to talk, or look in a shop window, or just stand staring up at the ceiling. Even my mother seemed to have slowed down.

When we got to the top of the steps leading up from the tracks, we both stopped, as if our batteries had suddenly conked out. Mom, I guess, was thinking whatever locked-away thoughts she'd had all the way here, while I scoped out the people around me, trying to find an Aunt Claire–type.

"There's nobody here," I said. "For us, I mean." I dumped my duffel bag onto a brown wooden bench.

"No, there wouldn't be," said Mom. "I just told Claire I'd get here as soon as I could. Come on, we'll get a cab."

We had started across the station, following the sign that

said TAXIS, when I was suddenly overcome by the smell of french fries. Wonderful, heavenly, crispy, crunchy french fries that made me double over with hunger. "Mom, wait. Can I get something to eat? I'll just grab it and take it with me."

My mother stopped, looking at me for a moment, then at her watch, and finally at the clock on the wall. "Oh," she said. "I wasn't even thinking. It's after ten—and you haven't had any dinner."

"That's okay, if I can just get a burger. I'll eat it in the cab."

"No," said Mom. "We'll go in and pick up something and sit at that table over there and eat it. Both of us. Besides, we're almost there and a little more time . . ."

As we placed our orders, I had a feeling that Mom didn't so much want food as she wanted to put off stepping out into this city where she hadn't been in seventeen years. I guess I was right about that because after we'd gotten our supper and found a table, I dug right in—to a hamburger, fries, and a Coke—while Mom sat staring at her tuna salad sandwich, poking it from time to time. As if she didn't know what it was.

"Mom," I said. "Let's just go. I'll wrap this up and—"

She shook her head, reaching over to take a french fry. "That's okay, Kiara. I think I need to sit here for a minute, to organize myself. But why don't you get some ice cream." She tucked a couple of dollar bills into my hand.

I didn't want ice cream because by then I was feeling half-sick, but I got it anyway, and ate it, and ended up feeling all-the-way sick. Not the barfing kind, but more the I-don't-know-what's-going-to-happen-next-and-what-do-I-do kind of sick. That's when I turned to my mother, looking for answers, and saw that she had slipped back into that faraway place.

I sat for a minute and then got up, bunched my trash together, and walked it over to the can. After that I slid Mom's tuna fish sandwich across to the spot on the table where she seemed to be staring, and said, "Do you want this now or should we—"

"Throw it away," she said.

"But you haven't—"

"Throw it away."

I did, and when I came back my mother was still looking at that same place on the squiggly green-and-yellow Formica table. That's when I touched her on the shoulder and said, "Mom, let's *go*."

It was a long cab ride, starting in the city part of the city and heading out past stores and parking garages, gas stations and bars. Next came houses in rows and houses with spaces in between and then houses with big spread-out lawns.

"We just keep going out Charles Street," Mom said, in a way that I'm pretty sure was to remind *her* of places she used to know, rather than to tell *me* where we were going.

"Johns Hopkins University," she whispered. And then, a little later, "Loyola College, and Notre Dame. And there's the cathedral."

Eventually the driver turned and started up a winding hill. "Main door where you want to go?" he asked.

"Yes," my mother said, reaching into her purse for her wallet. "Main door is fine."

The hospital was sort of flat, as if it were splattered there on top of the hill, and didn't look anything like the hospital in New York where I had my tonsils out. Inside, the lobby was wide and spacious, with wooden paneling and potted plants and big slouchy couches and chairs. It all looked as if it belonged in a resort hotel or motel except for the wheelchairs lined up by the door and the squawky voice on the PA system that from time to time would say, "Dr. Randolph, please answer your page."

Mom dropped her bag on a couch by the window. "Here, Kiara, you wait with our stuff and I'll find out where she is." Sitting on the arm of a chair and wishing I could settle all the way back and never move, I watched my mother head for the information desk and, once she was there, watched the man in charge point to a hall at the far side of the lobby and then perform an elaborate bunch of zigzag hand motions. I saw Mom's head going up and down, like one of those bobble-headed dolls some people have in cars.

"Now I remember about this place," she said, coming back to where I was waiting. "It's like a maze, or a rabbit warren. The first floor is really the third, unless it's that the third is really the first. Anyway, come on. We'll figure it out."

Yeah, sure, I thought. *I can see it now. The two of us lost in some hospital in Baltimore, doomed to wander the halls probably for days till we're eventually rescued by a security guard with a bobble-headed St. Bernard.*

And then, amazingly, my mother took off, and she was Lewis and Clark and Magellan and Marco Polo all rolled into one, as she made her way through the hospital in the middle of the night. With me running along behind, trying to keep up.

"Through the lobby . . . a sort of dogleg to elevator B . . . up and then along the corridor to the double doors . . . a right . . . and straight on . . ." She left a trail of words behind her.

I didn't know where we were going or how we'd ever find our way back, but suddenly we were there. *Somewhere.* And people crowded around us.

"Joyce, you're here," said a short woman with spiky gray hair and that same raspy voice I'd heard earlier on the phone. Which, I figured, made her Aunt Claire.

"I told you I was coming," said Mom.

"Yes, but we weren't sure—whether tonight or tomorrow— you know, with the trains and all," said another woman, who was a softer, rounder version of my mother. *Aunt Elinor,* I thought, as if filling in pieces of a puzzle.

There was a man with them, too, a sort of Ichabod Crane look-alike, and I had just about put him in the doctor slot when Aunt Elinor linked her arm through his and said, "Joyce, this is my husband, Ben. I don't think he was around when—I don't think you've met."

"Yes," said Mom, in a vague way that could have meant "Yes, we've never met," or "Yes, he's your husband," or "Yes, he wasn't around then."

Ichabod-Ben stuck out his hand, then yanked it back, and the four of them stood there as if trying to figure out whether to give each other those fake grownup air kisses or shake hands, or maybe just keep not quite looking at one another.

As for me, I felt so way-not-there that I was surprised to look down and see my regular feet and legs holding up my still-visible body.

That's when Aunt Claire stepped forward and caught hold of me on either side of my head and said, "Kiara," in one great swoosh of a breath. And kissed me on the forehead.

Then there were kisses all around, for me at least, and a bunch of stiff-armed hugs between my mother and her sisters. Then Uncle Ben shook Mom's hand, and mine, both at the same time. "Excuse my left hand, Kiara, and I'm glad you and your mother are here."

Once the kisses and handshakes and half-hugs were done, we all just stood there without saying anything. "Well, how is she?" my mother finally asked.

"Zenobia?" said Aunt Claire. "Not doing well. In fact, it's almost as if she's disappearing before our eyes. But so far the doctors haven't been able to figure out what's happening. One minute they say it could be only a matter of hours—and then, the next, that this could go on indefinitely. But let's go in so you can see for yourself. And remember, even if she doesn't respond, I'm sure she'll know you're here." She took Mom by the arm and started leading her toward a room with a half-open door. That's when my mother did her great Houdini escape act, freeing herself from Aunt Claire's hold and moving over to stand in back of me, digging her fingers into my shoulders.

"Wait," said Mom. "I mean, I'm not sure—after all this time. Maybe I should just stay out here—for a while, at least."

"It's time, Joyce. It's time for you to be here." That's when

Aunt Claire took hold of my hand and pulled us both into the room.

Except for having my tonsils out, I'd never really been in a hospital before, not even to visit. But one thing I knew straight off, this wasn't anything like in the Madeline book I had when I was little—with toys and dollhouses and rabbit-shaped cracks in the ceiling. This room was dark and shadowy with only a small lamp on the bedside table, its shade tilted so that its pale yellow light spilled into the corner. I tried not to breathe the air, which was sweet and sour and gross all at once. Even though my mother's fingers were hurting my shoulders, I didn't want to move away from her.

Gradually the woman on the bed came into view. Her body, under a white sheet pulled up to her neck, was long and bony. Her hair was white, matted to her head, and her face was sharp and fierce-looking. Her eyes were closed and her breath came in little gasps. And I found my own breaths coming in spurts to match.

Aunt Claire whispered something to my mother, but I didn't even try to make out the words. I didn't know this woman on the bed and all I *did* know was that suddenly I wanted to un-hook my mother's fingers from my back and run.

I think that up until this very moment, in some dumb kind of way, I'd still had the picture of the granny with the chocolate cake stuck in my mind—the one I described to the woman on the train.

Where was she? And who was this impostor in her bed?

4

Aunt Elinor got me out of there. I'm not sure how long I would have been trapped, with my feet glued to the floor and my knees shaking, if she hadn't taken hold of my hand and whispered to my mom, "Let go of her, Joyce. I'm taking Kiara."

We went down the hall to the waiting room, where Uncle Ben sat reading a tattered *Sports Illustrated*. "I don't think Kiara needed to be in there," Aunt Elinor said, nudging me onto a green vinyl couch across from him and settling down beside me. "Was I right?"

I nodded.

"It's hard," she said. "Claire brought your cousins down earlier, but I think they were all relieved when Frank took them back to the house. They're waiting for you there, by the way."

My eyebrows shot up and I crinkled my brow as I looked from one to the other.

"You don't know that you have cousins," Aunt Elinor guessed.

I shook my head. Suddenly I was mime-of-the-world, not at all sure that I could ever say regular words again.

"Your mother didn't . . ."

I shook my head again, then nodded, and finally managed to croak, "On the train, coming down tonight. She said something about her parents' grandchildren, but I never exactly thought of them as cousins, not the regular kind anyway."

"You mean regular like you see on holidays and visits and birthday parties?" said Uncle Ben.

"Uh-huh," I said, thinking of all the cousins on my father's side of the family, and the stuff we do together.

"Well, these guys are regular enough, and they're anxious to meet *you*." Uncle Ben held up four fingers and started counting them off. "First, according to age, there's Maddie, who's Claire and Frank's oldest. She's fourteen. Next comes our daughter, Jill—thirteen and just about your age."

"Followed by nine-year-old twins, Michael and Steven," put in Aunt Elinor. "They're Maddie's brothers—Claire and Frank's youngest. You *do* know that Frank is Claire's husband, don't you?"

Right about then I didn't know whether to keep saying *uh-huh* or remind them that up until today I'd never heard of any of these people. Which, I figured, would end up making my mother look far too weird. But suddenly it was as if I'd waded into a sea of tiredness and I didn't care who thought what about whom.

27

"I didn't know," I said. "I mean, I didn't know until this afternoon when Aunt Claire called that my mother had a sister, or another one, or even a mother. Because she never said, and I knew not to ask." I stared down at my fingers knotted in my lap, but even without looking up I could tell that Aunt Elinor and Uncle Ben were exchanging glances over my head, flashing some grownup kind of message.

Aunt Elinor reached over and untwisted my fingers, and Uncle Ben tapped me lightly on the head with his rolled-up *Sports Illustrated*. "Come on, Kiara," he said. "Let's you and me get out of here."

"Okay," I said, not caring enough to ask, *Out of here to where?*

He stood up, dropping his magazine on the table, and held out a hand to me. "I'll take Kiara on back to the house," Uncle Ben told his wife, "and you and your sisters can come later—whenever—in Claire's car. Okay?"

"Yes, that's a good idea. The three of us will probably just stay on here—until—you know . . ." Aunt Elinor blinked and looked away for a minute.

"Now," she said, turning back to face us. "Let's get organized here. Kiara, the girls are sleeping in the blue room on the third floor, toward the front of the house, and there's a bed in there for you. They'll likely be asleep, but you just go on in and settle down. Ben'll show you. And the bathroom's at the end of that hall—but be prepared. It's right out of another century and the shower's one of those handheld things, so just make sure the shower curtain's all the way around you and don't mind the way

28

the pipes rattle and clank. I put a clean towel and washcloth on the foot of your bed. And, Ben, you make sure Kiara gets something to eat before she goes upstairs. Claire got extra milk this afternoon and there're cookies in the cupboard next to the window and maybe a little turkey in the fridge if she wants a sandwich. Oh, and there's—"

Uncle Ben gently put his finger on Aunt Elinor's lips. "Don't fuss," he said. "Kiara will be fine. Now, you go on back to your mother. And tell Joyce I've taken Kiara."

"What house?" I asked after we had been driving for a while.

"What house what?" said Uncle Ben.

"What house—*whose* house are we going to?"

"Oh, I'm sorry. I thought you knew, but then I guess you wouldn't, would you? We're going to Fernhill, your grandmother's house."

"Her house has a *name?*" I asked. "I mean, is it just an ordinary house?"

"Fernhill is probably one of the most *extra*ordinary houses you'll ever see," Uncle Ben said, "but actually it *is* just an ordinary house. They do that a lot in England—name houses—and Lambert was quite taken with the idea, so when he and Zenobia bought the house, they named it Fernhill."

"Oh. Do you live there, too? And Aunt Claire and Uncle Frank?"

"Good grief no," said Uncle Ben, swatting at the steering wheel as if trying to do away with that idea. "Elinor and Jill and I live in Philadelphia, and Claire and her family in Virginia. But

29

when we got the call about Zenobia's fall, we came right away."

I nodded and looked out the window into the dark. "In what way is Fernhill an extraordinary house?" I said.

"You'll have to see that for yourself," Uncle Ben said as we started up a hill. When we got to the top, he turned left and we bumped our way along a narrow road before coming to a stop, with the car tilting sideways into a sort of gully. "Okay, let's go." He reached for my duffel bag. "But watch your step—it's dark out there."

I stood looking up at the house and thinking that it looked pretty regular to me. I mean, it was *big*, with giant trees towering all around, and a ton of steps leading up to the porch, where there was a glider and a couple of rickety-looking chairs off to one side. But still, it was just a house.

"Here's hoping Frank's awake," said Uncle Ben as he knocked on the door, then knocked again, even louder. "Or we may have to start throwing pebbles at the upstairs windows."

Uncle Frank, when he came to the door, was medium-tall and sort of stooped, with a round bald head that seemed to glow in the pale and watery light of the front hall. "Sorry, Ben. I must've dozed off. And who is this?" he said, leaning close and inspecting me.

"Frank, meet Kiara, Joyce's daughter," said Uncle Ben as we stepped inside.

Uncle Frank drew himself up and held out his hand. "Hello, Kiara. I'm here to officially welcome you to Fernhill."

"Thank you," I said. And then I noticed the room I was in, which seemed to have swallowed me up. It was a hall, really, but large and almost square. Just inside the front door there was a funky old coatrack draped with sweaters and jackets and hats and umbrellas with the spokes sticking out. Along one wall a double door was open to a room that seemed choked in shadow, while on the opposite side of the hall a steep flight of stairs led to the second floor. There was a huge copper kettle filled with dried thistly things, two small wooden rocking chairs, each occupied by a floppy, lonely ragdoll, and a one-eyed rocking horse with a scraggly tail. Two tables were heaped with books and bits of shapeless sculpture and an assortment of clocks, each telling a different time.

And the walls seemed to have sprouted paintings, which were hung side by side and one above the other, almost to the ceiling.

"Oh," I whispered. "It *is* an extraordinary house."

"Yes," said Uncle Frank. "And this is just the beginning."

I stepped back and turned around, squinting up at an oblong picture over the front door, but all I could make out was a faint gleam of yellow.

"You'll do better with this tomorrow, in the daylight," said Uncle Ben. "This is all your grandfather's work, and he was pretty adamant about what he would and wouldn't sell. After he died, Zenobia couldn't part with any of it, either, except on loan for the retrospective a few years back." He dropped my duffel at the foot of the stairs and went on. "Well, what do you think, Kiara? Do you want the tour, or how about that glass of milk Elinor was talking about? What'll it be?"

What I really wanted was to call my father, to hear his deep rumbly voice and tell him all that had happened since this afternoon. But I couldn't remember the name of his hotel in Boston, and besides, Mom had the cell phone with her. I thought about calling Granny Bee in Newark, but I wasn't at all sure I could ask to make a long-distance call from this extraordinary house. "No thanks," I said. "I think I'm just really, really tired."

"You're sure?" asked Uncle Frank. "There're chocolate cookies that seem to have appeared in the kitchen, and I saved some just for you."

I shook my head. "I can't—not now."

"Okay," said Uncle Ben, reaching for my duffel bag and starting up the steps. "Cookies tomorrow, bed now. Follow me."

And I did. Up the steps and along the darkened second floor and then up another flight to the third floor, where a tulip-shaped lamp hanging overhead cast spiky shadows out across the hall. Uncle Ben led the way to the room at the front of the house, standing back when we got to the door and motioning for me to go first. "Here we are," he whispered. "One of those lumps in those beds is your cousin Maddie, and the other is Jill. And this must be your spot." He put my bag on the floor next to a cot tucked into a window nook. "I think there's just enough light for you to find your toothbrush. If you're lucky. Now I'll show you the bathroom."

I followed him to a cavernous room with another tulip light suspended from the ceiling. There was a bathtub with fat claw feet, a toilet on a sort of platform, and a sink with knobby spigots that turned out to be animal heads—bear for hot and tiger for cold. A shower curtain hung from a small circular rod over the tub, and a coiled metal hose was draped across the soap dish. Which I figured was the handheld shower Aunt Elinor had told me about.

"Well, that about does it," said Uncle Ben. "Anything I can get for you? Anything you need?"

I need for it to be yesterday, I wanted to say. *I need to be back in New York with my mother and father. And I need never to have heard of any of these people or even this creepy house that's filled with shadows.* But "No thanks" is what I said. And "I'll be fine."

After Uncle Ben left, I dug my sleep shirt and toothbrush out of my bag and went back to the bathroom, where I took a totally weird shower, but I at least managed not to slosh water over the floor. The pipes rattled and clanked, the sink gurgled, and when I flushed the toilet, a swooshing noise roared through the wall behind it.

Back in the front room, a large black cat that hadn't been there before was sleeping on my bed. I tried pushing him one way and then the other, but he wouldn't budge, and I finally gave up and climbed in next to him, squinching my legs over to one side.

I lay there, suddenly wide awake, listening to my cousins breathing on the other side of the room, and thinking about my mother down at the hospital with the sisters she hadn't seen for seventeen years, and about the eagle-faced Zenobia, lying in that bed, still as a board. I felt shivery deep inside myself, and after a while I eased my legs over, curling them around the sleeping cat. I listened to his purring and studied a splotch of light from the hall until I fell asleep.

5

When I opened my eyes the next morning the cat was gone. The spot where he had been sleeping was still warm, though, which gave me a clue that the muffled thump I'd heard the minute before had been him jumping onto the floor. I propped myself up on one elbow and watched the light coming in the windows, which was both pink and gray at the same time, as if the day hadn't quite decided which way to go.

The walls of the room were lavender blue, like the inside of a shell, and were hung with old movie posters, tilting and slanting in all directions: *Gone With the Wind, Vertigo, The African Queen, The Wizard of Oz* . . .

I sat the rest of the way up, wrapping my arms around my legs and pulling my knees against my chest as I peered at my two sleeping cousins. The one in the farthest bed, a blonde, was sprawled on her stomach with her face turned away from me.

The other was curled into a ball, so that the only thing I could make out was a mop of red hair spilling onto the pillow. So much for checking out the relatives.

On the wall over the corner bed—the blonde's—were the words THIS IS JOYCE'S SPACE in black Gothic letters with a series of stylized red-and-yellow lightning bolts shooting out in all directions.

I caught my breath. *This is Joyce's space.* But Joyce was my mother. *Joyce's space?* And all of a sudden, for the first time since Uncle Ben brought me to Fernhill last night, I realized that my mother had actually *lived* in this house. That this must have been her room. That she would've probably put the words *This is Joyce's space* there on the wall, along with the jumble of posters. I could almost see her sitting cross-legged on that very same bed, where the blond-haired cousin was now, with a pot of black paint and a thin-bristled brush, carefully shaping the letters.

If this had been my mother's room, then did she have it all to herself? Or had the three sisters shared it? Claire, Elinor, and Joyce. And if they had slept here together, why—when there was the whole rest of this giant house? How long before she left had my mother written that on the wall over her bed? Had she ever been happy here? And, more important than anything, why did my mother leave and never come back?

Even though the room was warm and a little bit stuffy, I began to feel cold and creepy and wanted to get out of there. I fished clean clothes out of my duffel bag and picked up my flip-flops, then tiptoed down the hall to the bathroom. Which, if anything, looked even more dismal than it had the night before.

Once I had washed and dressed and worked (unsuccessfully) at flattening my hair with a wet washcloth, I made my way downstairs and along the second-floor hall.

It took forever for me to get the rest of the way to the first floor because I stopped on almost every step, looking at the paintings that lined the wall and filled the hall below. There was something strangely familiar about them, as if I'd known them from another time. The picture over the front door seemed to reach out and grab me, just as it had last night, and I went to stand beneath it, looking up.

It wasn't what my mom calls an abstract because I could tell right off what it was meant to be—a woman walking along a beach that stretched on and on until it ended in a mass of rocks jutting into the ocean. But it wasn't realistic, either, not like a photograph or a poster or even a postcard. Mostly what the painting did was *hint* at things, rather than shout them out loud, but all the things it hinted to I knew for a fact. I knew that it was late afternoon, or early evening, because of the way the light looked on the water. I knew that it was summertime, on account of the way the sand was that certain summer-gold and the woman's skin was dark, but from the sun and not like mine, which is that way all year round. And I knew, more than anything, that the cottage up on the dune would be worn and welcoming inside and filled with funky things. And that the woman, when she got to the rocks, would climb to the very top and sit looking out to sea.

I don't know how long I'd been staring at the painting when there was a sudden roaring noise deep within the house, and I realized that someone else was up, and either taking a shower or flushing a toilet. I looked around, not sure where to go, then reached to unlock the front door. As I started outside there was a swish of black fur between my feet and the cat pushed ahead of me, leading the way across the porch and around the side of the house.

That cat was gone when I got to the backyard, where he'd presumably disappeared into the stalky orange flowers that seemed to be running wild down one side of the grounds. The grass was cut, but just barely, and the rest of the place looked overgrown and untended. I'd lived all my life in an apartment building on the Upper West Side of New York, which definitely didn't have a yard, but one thing I like best about visiting Granny Bee in Newark is helping in her garden. All of a sudden my hands felt itchy, as if they wanted to start pulling up weeds and brambles and hurling them into a pile.

Instead, I wandered through the yard, stepping over a tangled hose and a row of empty flowerpots, plucking a dried geranium, then crushing it between my fingers and sniffing its half-icky smell before dropping it onto the ground. I stopped for a moment at an ancient swing—one of those wooden things with two seats facing each other—and gave it a push, watching as it glided back and forth. From there I moved over to a weathered green picnic table and settled onto one of the benches. I looked up at the house, at the rickety back porch and the open windows that seemed to gape emptily, like missing teeth.

Was my mother up there, in one of those rooms? What time had she come back from the hospital? And what had happened to *her* mother? Almost without thinking, I ran my fingers over the top of the table, tracing the dents and gouges in the wood. I noticed a bunch of letters which, at first, didn't mean anything to me until I managed to make out a curlicue *CJ*, an *EJ*, and the three chunky letters *JEJ*. "Claire, Elinor, and Joyce Elizabeth Jones," I whispered. Just then the cat jumped onto the table and, after giving me the once-over, stretched out and allowed me to scratch behind his ears. I sat there awhile, thinking how weird it was that bits of my mother seemed to keep turning up in this place that, until last night, I'd never known existed.

The cat dozed off but I went on scratching, mainly because there's something reassuring about cats' ears. I'm not sure how long we'd been there before I heard a *thwump* as a door opened and my cousins came outside.

"There you are," said the blond-haired cousin, as she stepped onto the back porch and caught sight of me.

"You and Eleven," said the redhead, as the two of them came down the steps and over to where I was sitting.

"Is that his *name*?" I asked, nodding at the cat.

"Uh-huh, they're all numbered."

"All?" I looked around the yard, as if dozens of cats were about to appear on tree limbs and trellises. "How many are there?"

"Only one, now. There was a calico named Ten, but he died, and stretching back almost forever and way before our time were Nine, Eight, Seven, and the rest," said the blonde. "Zenobia says that a name can inhibit a personality and numbering them leaves the cats free to evolve."

"She says that?" I asked, raising my eyebrows, then trying to flatten them down again.

"A lot. She says it a lot," the blond-haired cousin said as she sat down across from me and began stroking the cat.

"It's a wonder she didn't name our mothers A, B, and C, except I think she thought that evolving business was only good for cats," said the other cousin as she sat down next to me. All three of us were petting Eleven now, two pale hands and one like mocha latte on his coal-black fur. The cat, meanwhile, purred and seemed to smile a let-this-go-on-forever smile.

"I'm Jill," the blonde said after a bit.

"And I'm Maddie," said the redhead.

"And I'm Kiara Jones-Birkell."

"We know," said Jill. "We knew you were coming, so we waited up almost forever last night, until Uncle Frank sent us off to bed, and even then we swore we'd stay awake."

"Only we didn't," said Maddie, picking up Eleven and draping him over her shoulder, where he stayed for a minute, before jumping down and disappearing back into the flowers. "You've got cool hair, you know?"

"I hate it," I said, reaching up and making a sort of helmet with my hands, trying to flatten it down.

"Everybody does. Hate their own hair, I mean," said Jill. "Mine's lank and basically useless, and Maddie can't stand being a redhead."

"Makes me look like a walking bonfire, and when the twins are with me it's even worse. There ought to be some kind of a hair exchange."

"Yeah, where you could pass yours off and get somebody else's. And no matter what, you'd know it was only temporary." Jill pulled her hair back, and for a minute I imagined being able to reach over, borrow it, and plunk it down on my own head.

"Unless some bald guy came along and unloaded *his*," I said.

"Yeah, well, as an idea it might need some fine-tuning, but still . . ."

And then we were stuck, as if between the cat and the hair we'd used up everything there was for us to talk about, and it had suddenly occurred to us that we didn't really *know* each other.

"What happened last night? With your grandmother, I mean," I said eventually and mostly, I think, to end the silence.

"She's your grandmother, too," said Jill.

Part of me wanted to protest that *my* grandmother was in Newark, New Jersey, and probably at this very moment doing the crossword puzzle in her back garden. But that seemed tactless, and what Granny Bee would call ill-bred, so I hunched over the picnic table, running my finger over the dug-out *JEJ*, and said, "Well, ye-es, but did the grandmother—did our mothers come home, or are they still at the hospital?"

"Let's go see," said Maddie. "Nobody was up yet when we came out, but they probably are by now. C'mon."

The kitchen was long and narrow and looked as if it had

been stuck there on the back of the house almost by accident. And it was definitely crowded. Uncle Frank was measuring coffee into a blue-and-white speckled coffeepot while Uncle Ben shook cereal into bowls, and two bonfire-heads, whom I took to be Maddie's brothers, rooted in the refrigerator. They all seemed to be caught in a clutter of stuff: bunches of dried grass and flowers hanging over doorways, wooden masks lining the countertops, and a whole army of empty tomato cans stacked in a pyramid.

"Did Mom come back yet?" asked Maddie, leaning over her brothers to look into the fridge.

"No," said her father. "We haven't heard anything since Ben and Kiara got here last night, which, I'm sure, means there isn't anything *to* hear." He put the coffeepot on the stove and turned to me, saying, "Well, Kiara, I see you've already met two of your cousins. These two young renegades are Mike and Steve. Boys, this is Kiara." They each held up a hand for me to high-five, then settled onto a bench along the far side of the table.

"What's for breakfast?" asked Jill.

"Rice Krispies," said Uncle Ben. "Unless you'd rather have Rice Krispies. Or maybe even some Rice Krispies. We're a little low on provisions, and I'll have to make a store run later on, but right now those are your choices."

"Well," said Jill, "I think we'll have Rice Krispies." She handed bowls to Maddie and me, pushing the twins farther down on the bench.

As breakfasts go, it wasn't much. No toast or bagels or frozen waffles. Not even any juice. But I was so starving I didn't much care that the Rice Krispies had lost their snap, crackle, and pop and floated listlessly in the milk. Once I was finished, I leaned back, staring up at a mobile dangling from the high ceiling. "This really is a humongous house," I said.

"Yeah," said Jill. "Come on, we'll show you around—start at the top and work our way down. Except for our grandfather's studio, on account of Zenobia's kept it locked ever since he died." We rinsed our bowls and then headed through a narrow passage leading to the front hall. But no sooner had we gotten there than we heard the slamming of car doors out front, and without saying anything more, we waited for our mothers to come in.

6

The grandmother Zenobia didn't die after all.

My mother and her sisters stood in silence in that cluttery hall, looking gray and a bit shipwrecked. "What happened?" Maddie finally asked.

Aunt Claire shook her head, as if it were filled with pieces of a puzzle she was trying to put in order. "She woke up," she said. "She woke up and sat up and rattled the sides on her bed."

"And wanted to know what we were all staring at," added Aunt Elinor.

Mom steered Aunt Claire and Aunt Elinor into the living room, where the three of them collapsed onto the lumpy couch. Jill, Maddie, and I sat on the piano bench across from them.

"Zenobia?" said Jill. "She woke up? She's all right?"

"What's this?" asked Uncle Ben, coming in from the dining room, followed by Uncle Frank. "Did someone say that Zenobia regained consciousness? What—just before she d—"

"She woke up—came out of the coma—and she's still awake," said Aunt Claire, having another go at those puzzle pieces in her head. "It was the most amazing thing I've ever seen . . . I mean, everyone, including the doctors—especially the doctors—thought for sure . . ."

The twins suddenly appeared around the doorway to the hall, where, apparently, they'd been eavesdropping.

"You mean Grandmother Zenobia didn't die?" said Michael.

"And now we don't have to get dressed up and go to her funeral, right?" said Steven.

"But that's *good*, isn't it?" said Maddie, her voice cracking. "I mean it's *good* she didn't die, but you all are looking so totally bummed, and—"

"Of course it's good," snapped Aunt Claire, sounding more like herself. "It's absolutely amazingly good. It's just that I think we're all three in a state of shock. What with being up all night—and the waiting—and the stress—and then to have her just sit up like that, as if nothing untoward . . ."

If my mother and her sisters had looked shipwrecked before, they now seemed to be going down with the *Titanic*. And because right then I needed to be close to my mom, I did something totally weird. I went over and sat on her lap—which I only normally do when I'm kidding around and trying to convince her I'm as big as she is and could crush her bones to powder in a matter of minutes.

"What'd she say—your mother—when she woke up and saw you sitting there?" I asked. I had spoken softly, intending

44

the question only for my mom, but there was one of those dips in the conversation and my big-mouth voice rang out.

My mother sighed and wrapped her arms tightly around my waist. "She said, 'What are *you* doing here? Hoping to cash in on the inheritance?'"

"Welcome to the club," said Uncle Ben, laughing and slapping the side of his leg.

"Yes," said Aunt Elinor. "Zenobia says that at least twice every time we see her."

The rest of the day felt surreal. Mom and her sisters headed upstairs to bed. "Just let us get showers and some sleep, not necessarily in that order, and then we'll be fit to deal with all this," said Aunt Claire as they rounded the corner to the second floor.

The uncles took us kids out to lunch even though it was just eleven o'clock. We went to a Mexican place called Loco Hombre, where the food smelled unbearably delicious. The trouble was, even though I was starving, Mom hadn't given me any money, and I wasn't sure what to do about paying. Until last night Uncle Ben and Uncle Frank had never *met* me, so why should they *feed* me?

Uncle Ben must have read my mind because he handed me a menu and said, "Order up, Kiara. This is on Frank, so the sky's the limit."

That was when I discovered I love shrimp quesadillas. I think Uncle Ben was kidding about it being Uncle Frank's treat, though, since when the check came they split it down the middle.

From there we went to the Giant store, which is basically a giant supermarket—about fourteen miles from one end to the other. Things got a little hairy there, with Michael and Steven running up and down the aisles and coming back with things like frozen pizza and Hot Pockets and ice cream bars, and the uncles sending Maddie and Jill and me off to find where they came from and return them.

"Look, guys," said Uncle Frank, in aisle five, somewhere between pasta and rice. "We're only going to buy enough for the next couple of days—we can always come back. But first we'll have to find out what's going to happen, how long Zenobia will be in the hospital, whether she'll be able to go home to Fernhill, and how long any of us will be here. So let's put the brakes on this shopping, okay?"

From then on it was pretty basic: cereals, bread, milk, stuff for a couple of dinners. Uncle Ben pushed the cart and the rest of us trailed along behind, as if he were the Pied Piper or something. Until as an entire group we got to frozen food and the great ice cream debacle. It took only a couple of seconds for Maddie, Jill, and me to settle on chocolate chip cookie crumb, but by then the twins had something called bubble-gum cherry swirl already in the cart.

"No. That's totally gross," said Maddie. "And anybody who picks it is the grossest of the gross." She and Jill started making gagging noises.

"Yeah, but chocolate chip cookie crumb is booorrrrrring," said Michael.

"Boooorrrrrrring," chanted Steven.

"Enough!" said Uncle Frank. "We'll take both—and now let's go pay and get out of here. And next time Ben and I'll come shopping alone, and you all can stay home and tar the roof. Or whatever."

The most surreal part of the day happened late in the afternoon when we went to the hospital to visit Zenobia. That was because, now she had come out of her coma, the grandmother apparently was freaking out that no one was there visiting her. She had a nurse call twice, and then somehow she managed to put the next call through on her own. Aunt Elinor answered the phone and the whole time she was saying, "Yes, Mother," and "No, Mother," and I could hear this squawking in the background, like a chicken gone haywire.

"We'll be there in a little while," Aunt Elinor said. "Yes, Mother. *All* of us."

The hospital looked better in the daytime. Not at all eerie or shadowy, but busy and *purposeful*. And, with Aunt Claire sailing out in front, we seemed to get where we were going in no time at all. When we arrived at Zenobia's hall, a nurse hurried out from behind a desk. She looked worn and frazzled, which, I was beginning to suspect, dealing with the grandmother *did* to a person.

"She's been waiting for you," the nurse said, with a definite what-took-you-so-long tone in her voice.

"Well, we're here now," said Aunt Claire. "But because there're so many of us, we'll divide up and go in in small groups."

"NO," came a roar from inside Grandmother Zenobia's room. "Stop shilly-shalling in the hall and come in here. All of you. Now."

And we did. We crowded into the room, with Aunt Claire and Maddie and the twins moving over to the far side of the bed. I planted myself in back of Uncle Frank, peering around him to get my first look ever at Zenobia awake. She was as long and bony as I remembered her from the night before, with the same sharp and fierce face. What was different, though, was that her eyes were open and jet black, darting from one corner of the room to the next.

"A-ha," she said, seeming to shake her finger right through Uncle Frank and directly at me. "I see that brown little arm, so you'd better come out and let me have a look at you."

I froze—and might have stayed that way forever except that Jill grabbed me by the hand and pulled me out from behind Uncle Frank and up to the bed, standing next to me and keeping hold of my hand. "This is my cou—"

"Can't she speak for herself?" the grandmother asked.

I stood up straight and took a gulp of air. "I am Kiara Jones-Birkell, and I hope you're feeling better."

"What kind of name is that?" she asked.

"Jones for my mom, and Birkell for my dad, so people will know I'm part of both of them," I said.

"Do you take me for a fool? I figured that much out. It's the Kiara part—what kind of name is *that*?"

Her eyes seemed to bore into me, and just when I was thinking I maybe couldn't go on, Jill squeezed my fingers. "Kiara," I said. "It's Irish and it means 'little and dark.'"

Zenobia snorted. "Far as I know, you don't have a drop of Irish blood in your body. You're not little, and not as dark as I thought you'd be, though I can't say much for your hair."

"I'm the color of mocha latte, and my hair is my hair, and I think Kiara's a fine name." I stopped just short of saying *better than Zenobia*. But the weird thing was, I was pretty sure my grandmother knew what I was thinking.

"And you've got some spunk, I see," she said.

Jill seemed to recognize that last remark as a dismissal and pulled me back to stand with the rest of the family. *Well, she's not your regular kind of grandmother*, I thought. And I was pretty sure Mom was right when she said Zenobia wouldn't begin to know how to make a chocolate cake. I was so busy thinking all this that it took a while for me to tune in to the conversation swirling around me.

"I will *not* go to a nursing home," said Zenobia, rapping her knuckles on the tray table in front of her for emphasis. "Not. Not. Not."

"But, Zenobia—" Aunt Claire began.

"But, Zenobia—but, Zenobia—but, Zenobia," my grandmother mimicked. "Don't ever but-anything me."

"But—we spoke to the doctor this afternoon and he told us

about the Parkinson's—something you had never seen fit to mention," Aunt Elinor spoke quickly, trying to get in what she had to say.

"He's the worst kind of fool: one with a big mouth. And I'll have you know that I fell down a few steps, which has nothing to do with his so-called Parkinson's disease. And it's good I woke up when I did, or like as not, you all would have shoved me six feet under."

"Now, Zenobia, you just listen," Aunt Claire said, stepping closer to the bed.

My grandmother put her hands over her ears and began to hum.

"Just listen," Aunt Claire repeated, raising her voice. "We're trying to do what's best for you. Dr. McCardell says you had a nasty fall, and if the man hadn't been outside working on the porch roof, and if he hadn't heard you and gotten help—well, heaven knows what would have happened. Furthermore—"

"*Furthermore . . . furthermore . . .*" aped Zenobia.

"*Furthermore,*" Aunt Claire went on, her voice even louder, "Dr. McCardell says you're a mass of cuts and bruises, not to mention having a bad concussion, and it's just by the grace of God that, with the condition of your bones and all your other problems, you didn't break a hip. He says he's been telling you for years to get out of that house and—"

"Piffle." Zenobia put her head back against the pillows and closed her eyes. Just when I thought she'd fallen asleep, she opened them and glared at my mother. "Well, Joyce, as I recall, you always had plenty to say about everything."

50

"Claire's right," said Mom. "And Elinor, and Dr. McCardell. There's no way you can stay in that house—unless you had an attendant with you twenty-four hours a day."

"A zookeeper is an attendant," my grandmother said.

"There are all kinds of good places we can look into," said Uncle Ben. "Places that offer assisted living, but where you could still be independent and—"

"I don't remember asking your opinion," Zenobia said. She rested her head back again, feeling around on the bed for the call button, then jabbing it with her finger.

"Do you need something, Mrs. Jones?" The voice coming from the intercom was sharp and twangy.

"I need peace and quiet. Otherwise I'm contemplating a serious relapse. *Get these people out of here*," my grandmother said.

7

After being banished to the hospital corridor, we eventually made our way back to Fernhill, ate supper, served chocolate chip cookie crumb ice cream all around (because Michael and Steven found that bubble-gum cherry swirl was as gross as we *said* it would be), and cleaned up the kitchen.

The whole time we were doing all this—the cooking, the eating, the cleaning up—it was as if there were something hanging over us. The thing nobody was talking about yet. *What to do with Zenobia.*

"I'll see to getting the boys off to bed," said Uncle Frank. "And when I come down—"

"We can talk," finished Aunt Claire.

"And I'm sure the girls won't mind scooting out onto the porch while we have our discussion," said Aunt Elinor. "This really is just adult talk."

Now, even though I had only known Maddie and Jill since

that morning, there was already some kind of telepathy at work among the three of us. Maybe it was genetic, but no sooner had Aunt Elinor made that yuck-o "adult talk" comment than Maddie looked at Jill and Jill looked at me. Without being obvious about it, we all took note of the wide-open window from the living room to the porch.

"Yeah, Mom, we'll just scoot out to the porch and have a little *kid talk*," said Jill as we got up and headed for the door. Once we were outside, we lowered ourselves carefully onto this ancient, canvas-covered glider thing, easing back against the cushions. "Shhhhh," whispered Maddie. "If it creaks they'll hear us and close the window, so get comfortable and be prepared to not move."

We got ourselves all set for the great eavesdropping event, but for the next few minutes there wasn't anything much to hear except a little weather talk, a few sighs, and, from deep within the house, the clanging of a clock. I was beginning to notice every jab and prickle from the canvas seat covers, and had about decided that I'd never make it as a spy, when Uncle Frank came back into the living room and the conversation began.

"Well, the way I see it," said Aunt Claire in her most take-charge voice, "we have a real problem here."

"That's a masterpiece of understatement," said Aunt Elinor.

"And how would you put it, may I ask?" Aunt Claire's voice fairly hissed.

"Well, I—" Aunt Elinor started in but was interrupted by one of the uncles.

"All right," he said. "We know we have a problem. Zenobia's

health is such that it's impossible for her to live on her own, the Parkinson's will only get worse, and it's now up to us to decide what would be best for her. Okay?"

"That's my father," whispered Maddie.

"But all the while keeping in mind that Zenobia's hell-bent against going to a nursing home," added the other uncle.

"*My* father," whispered Jill.

"And you know, the way things are today, she'll be out of that hospital in no time."

"There is something called assisted living where they give help with bathing and medicines and all, but everyone has his or her own apartment."

"But it takes time to check those places out, and sometimes there's even a waiting list."

"Meanwhile, her coming back to Fernhill is out of the question."

The voices spun through the window onto the porch. The cushions were getting knobbier and pricklier by the minute, and I was just about to risk the screech of the glider by changing my position when I heard a question aimed straight at my mother.

"Well, Joyce, we haven't heard anything from you yet. What do you think?" asked Aunt Elinor.

"Zenobia and I—" Mom began. "I haven't been involved all these years, so I don't feel that I should—"

"You're involved now," said Aunt Claire. "And she's your mother, too."

"And still as mean as a snake," my mother said.

For a minute there was a conversation-stopping kind of silence that was broken by a bunch of non-comments.

"Well, yes, but . . ."

". . . the way she is . . ."

"You know Zenobia . . ."

". . . difficult, but . . ."

"Okay, then," said my mother, and I could imagine her leaning forward and hitting the edge of her hand on the table, the way she does when she wants to get something settled. "How about letting her come back to Fernhill and having help around the clock—at least until we can make other arrangements. Would that work?"

"It would give us time to find an assisted-living place," said Uncle Ben.

"It's asking a lot of the help—I mean, Zenobia's not always the easiest person to deal with," said Aunt Elinor.

"But the people who do this kind of work are special—they're trained to work with all kinds of patients," said Uncle Frank.

"It would certainly give us a chance to find something—and then talk Zenobia into it," said Aunt Claire in a that's-settled kind of voice. "We'll get started tomorrow trying to find home health aides."

"But those people aren't family," Aunt Elinor said. "No matter how good they are, we can't just bring Zenobia home from the hospital and dump her with a bunch of strangers."

"Well, who said anything about dumping?"

"Besides, we'll all check in from time to time. We'll call—and visit when we can."

"I'm not sure that's good enough."

"I'm scheduled to teach summer school this year, so . . ."

". . . can't just take off like that . . ."

"We have plans . . ."

Words and phrases shot back and forth, and I closed my eyes and saw my mother and her sisters, the way they must've looked about a zillion years ago. They were little kids in this very same room, in this very same house, and they were fighting about who had to wash the dishes. Or walk the dog. Or take out the trash. *I will . . . I won't . . . It's not my turn . . . It's up to you . . .*

I felt a sudden sharp jab in the ribs just as Maddie turned and yelled through the open window, "We'll do it. We're her granddaughters and we'll stay with Zenobia for the summer.

"C'mon," she said, grabbing hold of Jill and me and dragging us off the glider. And by the time we got inside it was as if this momentous decision involving summer and Fernhill had already been made.

We lined up on the piano bench again like those see-no-evil, hear-no-evil, speak-no-evil monkeys. "We'll do it," Maddie said again.

"Yeah," said Jill. "I mean, you guys are going to have help here anyway, so we wouldn't have to do the mediciney sort of stuff, but we'd at least be company for her."

"And Zenobia won't be stuck with just strangers," I said, ignoring the fact that until this afternoon Zenobia and I had been total strangers.

My mother picked right up on that, though, and said, "But, Kiara, you don't even *know* my mother. And besides, after all the problems—I don't think—"

"But, Aunt Joyce, she's Kiara's grandmother, too," said Maddie.

"And it has to be the three of us," said Jill.

"Yeah, Mom," I said. "And anyway, Dad would think I should stay. I know he would."

"It'll be cool. We'll entertain Zenobia and let her tell us about Granddad's paintings and walk down to the store and get whatever she needs. And play cards with her and all," said Maddie. Actually, the Granddad-painting stuff really interested me, but I wasn't too sure about the card-playing. Somehow I couldn't see Zenobia taking part in a fast-paced game of slapjack, but then, what did I know? Maybe she really was some kind of expert cardsharp in disguise.

"We can walk to the library, too," said Jill.

"And read all the books on our summer reading lists," I put in.

"But there's not even a television here," said Aunt Elinor, which was a completely baffling remark since adults are always saying that kids watch *too much* TV anyway.

"I can bring one from home," said Uncle Frank. "And hook it up for the girls."

The grownups proceeded to take over the conversation at

this point, and Jill, Maddie, and I wandered into the kitchen to polish off the rest of the ice cream—straight from the carton. Which everybody knows is the best way to eat ice cream. We were just finishing up when Mom came through on her way to the phone. "I'm going to call your dad, Kiara, and see what he thinks of this whole thing. I'm sure he'll want to talk to you."

After my mother disappeared into the little phone nook under the stairs, Aunt Claire and Aunt Elinor came in. "Why don't you girls go on up to bed," said Aunt Claire. "It's been a long day. And be sure and sleep on your idea about staying with Zenobia over the summer. If you still feel the same way in the morning, then we'll go over to the hospital and see what your grandmother thinks of the notion."

We did, and we did. Sleep on our suggestion, and feel the same way in the morning. As for what Zenobia thought of the idea, it was hard to figure.

Before we went back to the hospital, though, there was a whirlwind of activity the next morning, starting with me hunkering down in the telephone nook and having an in-depth conversation with my father. Mostly it had to do with commitment and had I thought this through and how once I got into it I couldn't just bail out and leave Maddie and Jill in the lurch. I guess I said all the right stuff because Dad ended up deciding our summer at Fernhill was a great idea and that he was proud of me. Which I'd figured he would—the great-idea part anyway.

"And remember, Kiara," he said, "your mom and I will be

coming down to check on you from time to time. After all, isn't it about time I met this grandmother of yours?"

Also that morning Aunt Claire spent absolute ages on the phone talking to this agency and that, then hanging up and telling Mom and Aunt Elinor and the uncles what they had said. By ten-thirty she had arranged for two health aides, each putting in a twelve-hour shift, to start work as soon as Zenobia got out of the hospital. Plus there was something about fill-ins on the aides' days off—or extra money if they worked straight through.

Meanwhile, Uncle Ben and Uncle Frank, with the help from the twins, were moving furniture out of the sunporch and taking Zenobia's bed apart and thumping it down the steps and setting it up where the moved-out furniture had been.

By eleven-thirty Mom, her sisters, Maddie, Jill, and I were at the hospital, walking into Zenobia's room.

"Well," the grandmother said, turning her head to the wall, "whatever it is you're coming here in battalion strength to tell me—I want no part of it."

"Oh, but, Zenobia," said Aunt Claire, "I think you'll want to hear this. Elinor and Joyce and I've come to present you with your companions for the summer." And with that she made some kind of funky parentheses thing with her arms around the three of us.

Zenobia put her hands up to her head, rubbing her brow. "I must be having some kind of fever dream," she said, pointing in our direction. "I thought I heard you say *these* were my summer companions."

"That's exactly what you did hear, Mother," Aunt Claire said. "We've all had an incredibly busy morning, and we've managed to arrange home health aides around the clock, starting as soon you as get home."

"And your three granddaughters didn't want you to be alone with just strangers, so they've offered to stay and keep you company," said Aunt Elinor, reaching out to smooth the sheet until Zenobia swatted her hand with a folded newspaper.

"The dark one, too?" the grandmother said.

"My name is Kiara," I said.

"And the redhead?"

"My name is Maddie."

"And the beanpole?"

"And *my* name is Jill."

"Hmmmph," said Zenobia. "I guess you expect me to babysit for them, don't you? Take them off your hands and get them into some kind of shape? And I guess *they* expect to be *paid*. Well, it's not going to—"

"You know that's not what we expect," my mother said, moving closer to me and putting her arm around my shoulder. "The girls are trying to do something to help, and it would be nice on your part if you could be a tiny bit gracious."

"Ahhh," Zenobia said, "the queen of nice has spoken. What I have to say is, you can install anyone you want in my house, but it won't help with the inheritance, so don't go thinking any one of them can weasel into the will. Your father set everything up before he died—a trust to take care of me for my lifetime, and after that it all goes to the Art Institute. Fernhill lock, stock, and barrel—and that includes your father's paintings. And I don't remember anything about the care and feeding of teenage granddaughters."

"We know, Mother," said Aunt Elinor, sighing. "You've told us for years. But the girls really do just want to help."

"There's help—and there's help," Zenobia said, pushing a button and lowering the head of her bed. "And the help I need right now is a brief rest before that slop they call lunch arrives."

Zenobia came home from the hospital on Saturday morning. Aunt Elinor and Uncle Ben went to get her, and when they got back to Fernhill, my mother, Aunt Claire, and Uncle Frank were waiting out front with a dining room chair and a long, skinny yellow scarf. Except for Michael and Steven, who were off in the woods at the end of the street, the rest of us were on the inside of the screen door, watching.

"Now, Zenobia," Aunt Claire said, reaching in to help her mother out of the car, "if you'll just sit on this chair and let us fasten this scarf around you, almost like a seat belt—"

"Sccccchhhhhee," hissed Zenobia, making a noise that sounded a lot like the one our cat, Gladiator, makes when we try to put him in his carrier.

"—then Ben and Frank will carry you up the porch steps," Aunt Claire went on, though her voice wasn't as certain as it had been when she started out. "They'll be very careful, and you—"

"No," said Zenobia, raising her arm and swinging her cane around and around, coming dangerously close to whacking Aunt Claire in the head. "I go where I go on my own—is that understood?" With that she brought her cane down, poked at the ground a few times, and made her way over to the steps.

My mother shrugged, Aunt Elinor fluttered, Aunt Claire ran up the steps and stood waiting on the porch. The uncles got into position behind Zenobia, I guess in case she came crashing down backward. And the grandmother concentrated on thumping her way into the house.

"Who are *you?*" she said, aiming her cane at the home health aide, who had already spent the morning getting a boatload of instructions from Aunt Claire.

"I'm Audrey, and I'm here to give you some help," the woman said.

"I have help," spit Zenobia. "I have Olivia, who comes over every Thursday to clean, and that's all the help I need. Those daughters of mine can't think of enough ways to spend my money."

"You are some lucky, Mrs. Jones. Some lucky indeed, because you're going to have Olivia-help and Audrey-help and nighttime-help, too," said Audrey, not quite smiling.

Maddie, Jill, and I had already decided that Audrey was cool, mainly because of the seven rings in one ear and the five in the other, and the blue-and-white speckled fingernails, but Zenobia obviously had other ideas. "I don't *need* help," she said. "And I don't like you."

"That's understandable—you don't know me. I'm not at all

sure I'm going to like you, either, but how about we both give it a try?" said Audrey, giving Zenobia a kind of you-and-me-alone-together-in-the-whole-entire-world look. But even as she spoke, she reached out and gently pushed the cane aside so that it ended up pointing at an empty birdcage and not at her. "One thing I do like, though," Audrey went on. "You've got some mighty fine paintings in this house—feel like I'm in a museum."

"Don't think you can walk out of here with any of them," Zenobia snapped. There were gasps all around as the rest of us stood staring at her. "I know exactly how many there are—and *where* they are," she added, a little smile sliding across her face as if she hadn't just said something so totally outrageous.

I stared at Audrey, but her face was as blank as a pulled-down window shade, except for a tiny twitch at the corner of her mouth. "Wasn't planning to walk out of here with paintings or anything else you might have," she said. "Ought to get that clear straightaway."

"What's wrong with them? My husband did these paintings. There are museums all over the world that'll fight tooth and nail for them—once I'm gone." Zenobia started to point her cane in Audrey's direction again, then seemed to think better of it and lowered it to the floor.

"Nothing wrong with them. I said I *liked* them, not that I planned to *steal* them. Now, you come along with me, Mrs. Jones. Your family's fixed up a grand-looking room for you, and we'll go and get you settled in before I rustle up a bit of lunch."

———

Zenobia didn't think the room we'd fixed for her was the least bit grand. Which ended up not surprising any of us. She wanted the bed here and the dresser there; this shade up and that one down; three pillows instead of two, but only if they had white pillowcases and not pink; and the lamp on *this* table switched with the one on *that*. And even then she wasn't quite sure, so that when all the arranging and *re*arranging was done, the room looked pretty much the way the uncles had it to start.

After the great room flap Audrey chased us all out, and the whole time we were in the kitchen making sandwiches I could hear the singsong rise and fall of her voice. It must've had some kind of (temporary) hypnotizing effect on Zenobia because I only heard her bang her cane a couple of times all that while. And then not with what Granny Bee would call gusto.

We ate lunch at the picnic table in the backyard, and Maddie, Jill, and I had only taken one or two bites before Aunt Claire was in full top-sergeant mode. And Mom and Aunt Elinor were right in there with her.

Do this . . .

Do that . . .

Be sure to . . .

And never . . .

We're leaving money in the samovar in the living room for any incidentals . . .

. . . be here on weekends . . .

Audrey and Rosa—she's the night aide—are in charge of all things medical . . .

There's a list of phone numbers on the refrigerator door . . .

Call if any . . .

The cleaning person comes Thursdays—but she's not to be picking up after you three . . .

And if there's a problem just . . .

Maddie, Jill, and I just kept nodding and saying "Uh-huh" with an occasional "We know" thrown in. We promised to do all the right things and not do the others and "to call at the drop of a hat," as Aunt Elinor put it, clapping her hands.

When everyone got up to clear the table, my mother caught me by the arm and said, "Kiara, come and take a walk with me out front so we can talk." We went down the street, around the giant pine tree in the middle of the circle, back up, and had started down again before Mom even opened her mouth.

"Now listen," she said, kicking a pinecone in front of her. "I think you're just being unduly stubborn about all this."

"All what?" I said in my super-innocent, who-me voice, guaranteed to push all my mother's buttons.

"You know exactly what I'm talking about, Kiara Jones-Birkell. Don't get wide-eyed with me when I'm trying to tell you something for your own good."

"But, Mom . . ." I rolled my eyes at the "for your own good" comment.

"Just listen for a minute," said Mom, "because I know right now you see Zenobia as some kind of cane-thumping, cantankerous cartoon character—with a sweet old lady inside just waiting to get out. But that's not the way it is. Not the way *she* is."

"But it's what I want to find out—how she *really* is," I said.

"Mean. She can be mean—and hurtful," said Mom. "She can be—"

"Besides, I *have* to stay. I promised Maddie and Jill, and we're in this together and we're—"

"Nobody can possibly expect you to stay here, given the circumstances. We'll just say that after thinking it over it'd be better if you went back to New York with me, and—"

"She's my grandmother."

"Oh? And when has Zenobia ever been a grandmother to you? Claire and Elinor know what happened all those years ago—how my parents made it clear that I was no longer a member of their family, that they'd never, ever—"

"Why did they? Do that, I mean. You never say. Even on the train coming down, you wouldn't say."

"Because I didn't do what they wanted me to do," my mother said, the words sounding rusty and unused.

"Which was?" I asked.

"Be my father all over again. It wasn't enough to have one renowned artist in the family, they needed two."

"Did your father feel that way, too?" I wanted to stop, to turn and face my mother, but we just kept on walking.

"You have to understand," said Mom. "My mother thought what my father thought. In all respects. If he said 'Jump,' she said 'How high?' If he had a headache, she took an aspirin. And when I dropped out of art school to marry your father—that was all it took."

"Because he was black?" I had to ask the question, still not sure I believed the sort of wishy-washy answer she'd given me on the train coming down.

"Black, white, green—I told you it wasn't completely to do with that. Black? White? I've never been sure. Maybe. Maybe not. The fact that your father was a black man didn't help, but the real, deep-down reason my parents reacted the way they did was because of the art thing."

"What art thing?" I asked.

For a moment I thought she wasn't going to answer me, but then my mother took a deep breath and said, "Sometime early on, when I was just a kid, my father decided that I had 'the talent,' and from then on I was forced to do *what was expected of me*. Once I figured out I could actually think for myself, it was—I was—to their way of thinking, giving it all up. Throwing it all away."

"But Aunt Claire and Aunt Elinor? What about them? They got married, and Zenobia's still—"

"They were the lucky ones," Mom said, kicking the pinecone so that it flew off into the bushes. "They couldn't draw so much as a stick figure. Nothing was expected of them."

We walked down the hill again and around the tree. After a while I reached out and touched my mother's arm. "I'm sorry," I said. "And I'm glad you did what you did. But I still need to stay. These are my cousins, and I want to get to know them. Zenobia is my grandmother, no matter what, and she's—"

I stopped, not sure what to say next, and my mother and I made another whole circuit around the tree before she sighed and said, "Okay, Kiara—okay. If you're sure." Then, after another half loop, she added, "If you're going to be here awhile, I guess you'll be needing more clothes and things. I'll send them when I get home."

The next twenty-four hours went by in a whirl, and trying to reach back inside and pluck out actual events is a little like reaching into a grab bag. One thing, though, was that Uncle Frank went home to Virginia to pick up a TV and VCR for us and hooked them up in Zenobia's living room. But no sooner had Michael and Steven settled down to watch the Orioles game than Zenobia sent a message by way of Audrey: "Turn it down, or I'll have the power shut off."

Uncle Ben got Chinese carryout for everyone except Zenobia, who said, "All it is is snow peas and bok choy—and if I wanted *that*, I'd eat in a field."

Rosa, the night aide, arrived after supper, and Audrey went home, and from then on, the level of cane-thumping went up a hundredfold.

And when I awoke in the middle of the night, with just the pale yellow light from the hall edging into the room, I was pretty sure Maddie and Jill were awake, too. None of us said anything, but I'd bet a million dollars that we were all thinking the exact same thing: *WHY are we doing this?*

The next day got even whirlier. There were last-minute everythings: trips to the store, phone numbers taped to the fridge, and instructions, instructions, instructions. The twins brought down the suitcases, and the uncles packed the cars. Fi-

nally everyone crowded into Zenobia's room to say goodbye—
the aunts, the uncles, the twins, along with the three of us who
were staying. My mother stood as far back as she could get,
pressed up against a bookcase with a moldy stuffed owl on
the top.

"Now, Mother," Aunt Claire began. "One of us will be here
the end of next week, and meanwhile we'll be hard at work to
find someplace—some really suitable facility—"

"Go!" shrieked Zenobia. She turned away and with the side
of her arm swept everything off the table in front of her. Glass
broke, water spilled, and pill bottles rolled across the floor.
"Go!"

Maddie, Jill, and I sat on the porch and watched the cars de-
parting: Aunt Claire, Uncle Frank, and the boys heading for
Virginia; Aunt Elinor and Uncle Ben to drop my mother at the
train station and then go on to Philadelphia.

A creeping emptiness was folding itself around us. We sat on
the glider, not moving, until Maddie reached out and dug the
fingers of her right hand into my left leg, and the fingers of her
left hand into Jill's right leg.

"Yeah," said Jill.

"I guess," I said, though I didn't have a clue what I meant.

"Okay," said Maddie.

Just then the *thwack-thwack-thwack* sound of the cane came
through the living room window. "All right," called Zenobia.
"You three said you were going to be here all summer, scroung-

ing on my generosity and with some trumped-up excuse about entertaining me. So come in here and entertain."

Our entertainment turned out to be a total disaster, especially when Jill asked Zenobia whether she preferred rock or rap. This led to our grandmother calling us "empty-headed imbeciles" and throwing a potted African violet across the room. "Get out of here," she said, her voice suddenly low and steely, "and let me contemplate alone what is bound to be the worst summer of my life."

"Ditto," said Maddie as she and Jill and I made our way to the third floor. "Ditto, ditto, ditto."

9

Rosa didn't show up that night. The agency sent Barbara in her place, who didn't show up the night after *that*, and who was replaced by Corinne, who, like the ones before her, lasted a twelve-hour shift. Then came Lily, Margaret, and Gwen.

Six home health aides in six nights.

Next Ada arrived. She was small enough to walk under the mantel without it grazing the top of her head and had moppy black hair, with traces of green. The muscles in her arms and legs were hard and knotted like those of my sixth-grade music teacher, who'd been a ballet dancer before she became a teacher.

"Are you a dancer?" I asked.

Ada guffawed. That's a word I've seen in books a bunch of times and never, in a million years, thought I'd use. But Ada really did guffaw. "*Me*? In a *tutu*?" she gasped when she finally caught her breath.

Then, after shaking hands all around and having a mini-conference with Audrey on the front porch, she went in to Zenobia's room, closing the door behind her. None of us will ever know what took place in there, but from then on, Zenobia pretty much stopped hurling plates and books and trays. Same as she'd stopped pointing her cane at Audrey.

"We had a meeting of the minds" was all Ada would ever say.

After that first night, Audrey and Ada took to having a regular confab on the porch as one was coming and the other was leaving, to give each other updates about how the grandmother was doing. They started calling themselves the A-team.

If Ada and Audrey were the A-team, Maddie, Jill, and I were definitely the Z-team. Or lower. I can't swear to this, but I'm 99%/10 percent sure that, like me, Maddie and Jill were wishing that we could all three just walk out of there one morning—and keep on going. And that an agency somewhere would send in replacement sets of granddaughters. A Meg and Cindy and Erin, or maybe a Susan, a Kate, and a Sharon.

There wasn't any such agency, or any stand-in granddaughters, either, which meant that we were stuck with Zenobia, and she was stuck with us. Meanwhile, no matter what we did, it was wrong.

If Maddie and Jill and I decided, early in the morning, that we'd spend the whole day being sweet and docile and never once let Zenobia get to us, the plan was sure to backfire by 10 a.m. That's about how long it took for Zenobia to start thwacking everything in sight with her gnarly fists and shouting, "What did I do to deserve a gaggle of such colorless, wimpy grand-daughters?"

If we vowed, the next day, to be strong and assertive, it wasn't long before our grandmother described us as mouthy, cheeky, and disrespectful to our elders.

If we set out to entertain her, we fell flat on our faces. And if we escaped to the front porch, listening to the crickets and trying not to think about how grossly hot and humid it was, we were accused of being feckless ne'er-do-wells who wouldn't amount to a hill of beans.

When Audrey went to the grocery store and came home with a half gallon of peach ice cream, Zenobia said if she'd wanted peach ice cream she'd have *asked* for it. That she actually *hated* peaches, and there was a good chance she was allergic to them. But no sooner had Jill, Maddie, Audrey, and I finished off the carton than Zenobia demanded a bowlful—of peach ice cream.

Then there was the thing about the television set. Zenobia seemed to have supersonic ears and claimed it was blaring in her room while the rest of us were huddled over the set in the living room, trying to lip-read what the actors were saying. Apparently TV was something else Zenobia hated—until we suggested moving it to the third floor so it wouldn't disturb her. That's when she took to thumping and caterwauling and asking, "Just how do you expect me to get to the third floor in the event there's ever anything I *choose* to watch? Explain *that*, if you will."

"Was your grandmother always like this?" I asked one afternoon, as Jill, Maddie, Audrey, and I sat on the front porch eating ice cubes.

"Our," said Maddie.

"Our what?"

"Grandmother. She's *yours*, too," said Jill.

"Yeah," I said, shifting my ice from one side of my mouth to the other and wondering if Zenobia had ever heard of air-conditioning. "But was she? Always like this?"

"Uh-huh," said both of the cousins at the same time.

"Bossy and pretty much wanting everything to be her way," explained Jill.

"She took us to New York once, to see the retrospective of our grandfather's paintings, and she spent a lot of time shaking her umbrella at cabdrivers and fussing with the doorman at the hotel," said Maddie.

"Yeah, and she followed people around the exhibit and listened to what they had to say about the pictures and then told them what they *should* have been saying," said Jill. "But, if you ask me, she's gotten worse. You know, crabbier and all."

"She was crabby to my mother, way back. Mean, actually. Both Zenobia and the grandfather," I said. "And made her not be part of their family anymore."

There was an incredibly long silence after that, filled mostly with the sound of us all crunching ice cubes. "We knew we had a cousin and she lived in New York," said Maddie. "And one night, when we were there for the retrospective and Zenobia was taking a bath, we looked in the phone book and were going to call you and see if we could all just manage to run into each other, sort of accidentally on purpose. Except that there were a zillion Joneses and we didn't know which was which."

"And we knew enough not to ask our grandmother," said Jill.

Then there was another stretch of silence until Audrey finally said, "People do that, you know. Get to be more of what they're like as they get older. So watch what you are *now*."

"But does she have to be mean?" I asked. "Granny Bee's not mean. Or my grandfather, either. Nor really anybody else I know."

"Did it ever occur to you girls that your grandmother might be scared?" said Audrey. "I remember once when I was little being so afraid at the dentist's that I bit his hand."

"Yeah, but you were a kid and Zenobia's a *grownup*," said Maddie.

"What?" said Audrey, moving from the porch railing to a rickety wicker chair. "You don't think grownups get scared? Of course they do. Plenty of times. It's just that part of being a grownup means that A, you've learned to deal with whatever it is you're afraid of, or B, you've figured out how to cover it up."

"So you don't bite the dentist," said Jill.

"Yeah, but what's Zenobia scared of?" said Maddie.

"You tell me," said Audrey. And then, when none of us said anything, she went on. "Okay, how's this for starters. She's getting older, her husband's dead, she has Parkinson's and is beginning to shake, and she knows, in her heart of hearts, that she has

76

to move out of this house. But she doesn't want to—and she doesn't know where to go. And despite what she says, she's probably lonely."

"But when people call, she won't let them come over," said Jill, "and when they send cards and stuff, she throws them away."

"So you're saying that Zenobia bites with words," I said, turning to Audrey. "Except—how come she was so mean to my mom? What was she afraid of back then?"

When nobody answered me, I went ahead on my own, putting into words a bunch of what I'd been trying to understand. "Unless she was scared that she couldn't keep control and all along she wanted my mother to be a famous artist like the grandfather—but Mom wanted to do what Mom wanted to do. Which she did, and which involved dropping out of art school and marrying a black man. Which maybe freaked her parents out."

"Yeah," croaked Jill. "But people aren't *supposed* to control other people. Or be freaked out by who their kids marry, either. It's not *fair*."

"You're right, Jill. It's not," said Audrey. "But this isn't a perfect world, and I hope I'm not destroying any illusions here, but—some people just start out meaner than others. And remember what I said about becoming more of what you are."

"You know what?" said Maddie. "The thing with Zenobia and us, well, it's like Doctor De Soto—you know, the little mouse dentist in that picture book—and how he had to treat the fox or the wolf or whatever he was—"

"And how he was always waiting for the fox to chomp down on him," said Jill.

And I think at that moment, Jill, Maddie, and I saw ourselves as a trio of Doctor De Sotos, all trying to deal with Zenobia the fox.

And, for some totally weird reason, it helped.

10

What Jill and Maddie had said about Zenobia taking them to New York to see their grandfather's retrospective kept jiggling around in my head all the rest of that day and long into the night. I slept and didn't sleep, never quite able to shake the feeling that I knew something I didn't know I knew. As if vague, wispy clues were dangling in front of me, but every time I reached for one it poofed away into nothingness.

Then, in the middle of the night, I shot up out of bed, dumping Eleven, who was sleeping across my feet, onto the floor with a thud. I was goose-bump shivery, even though the third floor at Fernhill could have passed for a sauna, and when Eleven jumped back into my lap, I wound the sheet around us both.

And suddenly I was nine years old again, going with my mother to the Whitney Museum to see an exhibition. There was nothing so odd about that—Mom and I went to a lot of art shows, in regular museums and posh, whispery galleries and funky, far-out kinds of places. My mother would keep up a running commentary wherever we went, trying, as she said, to teach me "constructive looking." She'd throw out terms like "vanishing point" and "impressionism," and "pentimento," which I used to say over and over just because I liked the way it sounded. *Pentimento, pentimento.* And "chiaroscuro," too, 'cause it sort of sounds like Kiara.

And she would ask me questions. What did I see? What did I feel? What did the artist *want* me to see?

But that day at the Whitney was different. There were no conversations, no questions, not even any time spent on my art education. In fact, except for turning around from time to time to make sure I was still there, it was as though my mother felt she was the only person in the museum. As if the bunches of people crowding the galleries didn't exist.

Looking back, I realized that the show Mom and I saw at the Whitney that day was the same show Maddie and Jill had gone to New York to see. That the artist was my mother's father. *My* grandfather. Finally I understood why Lambert Jones's paintings had seemed so familiar when I first arrived at Fernhill.

If things had been jiggling in my head before, they were positively leapfrogging now. Thoughts tumbled over thoughts, followed by what-ifs and what-might-have-beens.

Maddie, Jill, Zenobia, Mom, and I might possibly have been in different parts of the museum at exactly the same moment. What if Mom and her mother had rounded a corner and run smack into each other? Would they have stood back, and looked, and laughed, and then run into each other's arms? Or would they have been iffy and prickly and maybe even walked away from each other? And why were things the way they were between my mother and her mother; between my grandmother and her daughter? I knew what Mom had told me, and I believed her, but still . . .

None of this made sense, and the more it didn't make sense, the more I tried to figure it out. All the way through the night. I tossed and turned so much that Eleven gave up on me completely and moved over to Maddie's bed. In the early morning I lay listening to the racket of the birds in the maple tree outside the window and the little huffing noise Jill made when she slept, and watched the sky go from gray to pink to blue. And when it was time to get up I was headachy and pretty much felt like the walking dead.

Things didn't improve with breakfast, and when Audrey suggested that Maddie, Jill, and I walk down to the library and then stop at the store and pick up the things on the list she was waving in front of us, I let out a groan and clunked my head back against the wall. Which didn't help the headache any.

Audrey reached over to touch my forehead, her blue-speckled nails feeling like ice chips against my skin. "You're not feverish, but you sure look like something the cat dragged in. So okay, we'll move on to plan B. Maddie, how about you and Jill go off to the library and the store, and Kiara can hang out here, and maybe even have a little quality time with your grandmother."

"Quality time?" The three of us turned to look at Audrey as if we were operating with one head. I mean, "quality time"

wasn't exactly her kind of phrase, but before I could even react Jill blurted out, "You've *got* to be *kidding*."

Audrey pushed herself away from the table. "One can only hope," she said, with just the slightest twitch of her left eyebrow.

Before Jill and Maddie left, we did a bit of editing to Audrey's grocery list, adding Mint Milano cookies and veggie chips. I also put in my request for library books: "Nothing soppy, and something so incredibly good that if I've already read it I won't mind reading it again." Then I sat slumped on the front porch and watched them go up the hill.

It was one of those summer mornings when everything feels muffled and drifty and far away. Whatever sounds there were seemed to lump themselves together and roll over me—the hum of a lawn mower, a truck at the top of the hill, a telephone ringing somewhere. My head dropped forward, onto my chest, and I was just drifting into a delicious sleep when a sudden rapping sound yanked me back. My eyes shot open, and when I spun around there was Zenobia, looking at me through the window between the living room and the porch.

"I know sloth when I see it, and I don't like it," she said, rapping on the sill again. "What—you're too *good* to walk down to the store with your cousins, or just too *lazy*?"

"I—wha—I—" There was so much I wanted to say back to her, but the words tangled inside my head. Before I got them sorted out, Audrey appeared in the open window next to Zenobia.

"Nothing lazy about this young lady, Mrs. Jones. Or slothful either. Matter of fact, we planned it this way. Thought you'd like to spend a little one-on-one time with each of your granddaughters," she said, winking at me over Zenobia's shoulder.

"Can't see any reason why I'd want to do that," my grandmother told Audrey. "One-on-one, hmmmph. Next you're going to tell me it's *quality time* or some other nonsense." But then she said to me, "Well, get in here, girl, and we'll see what we have to talk about."

I dragged myself up off the glider and into the house as slowly as I could, through the hall and living room, and back to the sunporch/Zenobia's room, where she had settled into her favorite Morris chair. Her cane was across her knees, her head resting on the back of the chair, and as I came into the room she muttered something that sounded a lot like *sloth*.

The words I couldn't find before came tumbling out. "I'm not lazy and I'm not a sloth and neither are my mother and father. They both work really, really hard, and my dad's written eight books and won all kinds of awards, and my mom's written one and—"

"Oh?" interrupted Zenobia. "Your mother's written a book, has she? On what—*How to Waste Your Life and Talent in One Easy Lesson?*"

"It's about bears, and it's a picture book and it got fantastically good reviews with stars on them and *The New York Times* said they looked forward to more work 'by this talented artist.'"

"*Bears?*" said Zenobia. "*Artist?*"

With that I was up, racing to the third floor, where I grabbed Mom's book out of the bottom of my duffel bag, and tearing back down. I knew there'd been a reason I'd packed it.

"See," I said, struggling to catch my breath. "Here it is—and I don't see why you have to be so mean."

"Ah. A spirited defense, I see."

"Why *do* you? Have to be so mean?" I pushed.

"I am what I am, but I don't like waste. Your mother could be shown in the finest galleries and instead she's dabbling in *bears*," Zenobia said. "In a *children's* book."

"But it's so good, and you haven't even looked at it," I said, waving the book as close to her face as I dared. After a bit Zenobia reached out and took the book, handling it with two fingers and dropping it onto the table, as if it were covered in some kind of slimy fungus she couldn't stand to touch.

"What you don't understand, girl," she said, wiping her fingers down the side of her skirt, "is that more is expected of those who are given a great gift."

"But why is it up to you?" I said. "My mom has a gift—for telling stories and drawing pictures—and she uses it all the time. But what if she didn't? What if she wanted to be a waitress— that's a gift. Or sell pizza at the mall, or drive a bus, or cut hair. They're all gifts, so why is it up to you what anybody else does?"

"Is this the way you were brought up—to disrespect your elders?" said Zenobia, giving the table a slight nudge as if to shift Mom's book as far away as possible. "Is that considered pre- cocious? Or just modern and ill-mannered and somehow desir- able?"

I wanted to tell her *she* was the most ill-mannered person I'd ever met. I wanted to grab my mother's book and wipe Zeno- bia's fingerprints off with my shirttail. And most of all I wanted to get up and slam out of that room. Instead, I clenched and unclenched my toes inside my tennis shoes and took a long, deep breath before I said, "No, I wasn't, and I don't. Disrespect my elders, I mean. Or anybody else. Except I would—I'd have to—if someone was really obnoxiously mean to my mother, who was this person's very own daughter, and had a grand-daughter she'd never seen even once in thirteen years and on account of this the granddaughter didn't even know she *had* another grandmother until this very summer. And if she—this person—had a perfectly good son-in-law she hasn't ever met."

I held my breath to see what Zenobia would say, but she seemed to be concentrating on picking some nappy little lint balls off the sleeve of her sweater. One, and then another, and another. "Hmmmmmmph," she said after a while, then went back to her delinting. But just as I was concluding this one-on-one visit had come to an end, she cleared her throat and said, "Your father is a man who honors his talent."

"My fa-father?" I choked. "You've heard of my father?"

"Do I look stupid?"

"Have you read his books?"

"Of course," said Zenobia. "And, as I said, he honors his talent."

"Yes, *but*," I added, "he also honors my *mother's* talent."

"Bears?" snapped Zenobia, as if it were a dirty word.

"Same as he'll always honor mine, when I figure out whether to be an actor or a veterinarian or a photographer and get to go to really exotic places," I said.

My grandmother made a face and curled her top lip. She

85

rubbed her hands together as if washing them without any water, sighed, and said, "Your mother could have done something worthwhile. She could have been one of the great ones."

And right away, listening to Zenobia start in on that again, I felt like a gerbil or a hamster or whatever it is that runs around and around on one of those little wheels. I was just trying to figure out how to make my escape when Audrey came in with Zenobia's medicine and said, "I see the girls coming down the hill, Kiara, so why don't you go and meet them."

I gave her one of those I'm-eternally-grateful-and-will-be-for-the-rest-of-my-life looks and headed out the door.

Sometimes I think Audrey has ESP.

11

The next day Audrey desperately needed Minute rice from the store. (It didn't take long for the three of us to figure out that Audrey was going to have a new desperate need every day—her way of getting two of us out of the house and giving us a break. And making sure the other had that dreaded one-on-one visit with Zenobia.)

Anyway, that day Maddie and I headed down to the shops, kicking stones and pinecones as we went, and generally taking our time. It's a known fact that it doesn't take long to buy one box of Minute rice, so we told ourselves that we were aliens from another planet who had just landed and been sent out to reconnoiter for food. That's how we got to walk in and out of three hair salons, an ice cream parlor, a used-clothing store, a jewelry boutique, a bank, and an antiques shop. Each time we came out shrugging our shoulders and saying, in our best alien voices, "No rice there."

It's amazing what being bored out of your skull will make you do.

We finally worked our way down the shopping area to Henley's Market, picked up the Minute rice, and went home. The two of us, somehow, managed to kick the same stone to within half a block of Fernhill, when it went spinning down the storm drain.

"You *guys*," said Jill when we found her slumped under a bush on the front lawn, tears running down her face. "Where *were* you?"

Maddie and I looked at each other, alien voices ringing in our ears. "Oh, you know," said Maddie, "it takes a while, getting down there and all."

"And Henley's was sort of crowded," I said, "and then we had trouble finding the Minute rice, and—"

"It was really backed up at the cashier—"

"You *went* somewhere, didn't you? For ice cream, or a soda?" said Jill, rubbing her eyes and crawling out from under the bush.

"Nuh-uh," Maddie and I both said, shaking our heads virtuously.

"Or else you just really dragged your feet—on purpose," Jill went on.

"Well, sort of," I said, digging into the grass with the toe of my shoe.

"I guess," said Maddie. "But how was it with Zenobia?"

Jill looked over to the front porch, in case Zenobia was lurking by the screen door, then beckoned for us to follow her into the backyard.

"What happened?" I asked as we settled around the picnic table.

"Everything—and nothing," said Jill, picking at one of the initials in the tabletop. "It's just that she's wicked, and evil."

"And mean as a snake, my mother says," I added.

"But what *happened*?" said Maddie. "Did you talk? Did you ask her questions or get her to tell—"

"How can you talk to a barracuda? And then I saw Kiara's mom's book sitting there, and I made the mistake of picking it up and starting to read it out loud, and Zenobia pitched a fit and told me to get out, and when I started to, still with the book in my hand, she said what was I—a thief? And to put it back where I found it, it belonged to her. And just think, to-morrow it's *your* turn," Jill said, pointing to Maddie. "And Kiara and I are going to take *forever* getting back. Just you wait."

"Okay," said Maddie, twisting her hair into a ponytail. "That's fair enough. But I can tell you one thing: Zenobia's not going to make *me* cry."

Maddie didn't cry after her visit with Zenobia. She broke out in hives instead. When Jill and I got back from our (slow) walk to the shops for one can of chicken noodle soup and more Mint Milano cookies, we found her on the front porch. Scratching.

"They itch, and they're swelling up," said Maddie, digging at her forearm. "Tell me there aren't any on my *face*."

Jill and I stared at Maddie's face—at the angry red blotches, the eyelids puffed almost all the way closed, the swollen lower lip that twisted her mouth in a weird sort of way. "We-ll, we could tell you that, but it wouldn't exactly be true," said Jill.

"Oh, no. You mean they're *there?*" moaned Maddie, rubbing her fingers carefully over her face as if she were dealing with unfamiliar territory. "What'm I going to *do?*"

"Isn't there something—some medicine that'll take them away? Jill and I'll walk down to the store and get it. I mean *really* walk, fast and all and not stopping for anything," I said.

"Thanks, but uh-uh," said Maddie. "Audrey called the pharmacy to refill one of Zenobia's prescriptions, and they're going to send a tube of some stuff that might work for hives."

I watched Maddie scratching her knee and then her ankle and her elbow, and suddenly I felt itchy all over. "Do you get them a lot? Hives, I mean."

"Never. I was just sitting there in Zenobia's room listening to her harangue about young people today and lack of perseverance and sloth and general indolence, whatever that is, and my legs suddenly felt like they were on fire and started itching, and I looked down and they were like this. I didn't even know what they were till Audrey told me."

"Did you get her talking about anything else, before the sloth and indolence bit?" Jill asked.

"I tried. I started out by telling her about Michael and Steven—I mean, they *are* her grandsons—and how one of them wants to be an astronaut and one a policeman, except that it keeps changing as to who wants to be which. And how I'm going to write these incredibly good books, like Kiara's father, and maybe even almost win a Pulitzer Prize. Then I asked Zenobia what she had wanted to be when she was a little girl. If she ever was a little girl, though I didn't actually say that part. And she said Lambert Jones's wife."

"Did she *know* him when she was little?" I asked.

"That's what I said," Maddie went on. "And she told me that was a ridiculous question, that of course she hadn't, but some things you just know. She called it karma. And from there she went into the sloth and lack of perseverance mode."

"And indolence," I said. "Which I think is a lot like sloth."

The next day it was my turn with Zenobia again. (This time Audrey needed two tomatoes and a sprig of parsley.) After Jill and Maddie left for the store, I sat on the front steps for a few minutes, remembering something Granny Bee said a lot. About how a smile starts with another smile. That's when I decided that all it would take to turn Zenobia into the granny I wanted her to be, or at least get her halfway there, was a healthy dose of grins and positive thinking. So I stood up, plastered an ear-to-ear smile on my face, and went into her room.

"What are those silly things on your feet?" my grandmother said. "I hope you don't call them shoes."

"Well, they're flip-flops, but yeah, I guess they're shoes." I stretched my smile even wider.

"Not that I'd expect much better, but your mother lets you go out in them?"

"Some places, yes. And the cool thing now is that my feet

91

are the same size as my mother's, so I can wear her flip-flops, too, which gives me twice as many." It was hard to talk with that grin firmly in place, but I managed.

"Hmmmmmph," snorted Zenobia, giving up on my feet and looking me all over. "Is there something wrong with your face? The one in here yesterday broke out in welts and now you seem to be twitching around the mouth."

So much for a smile leading to another smile. I let my face go back to normal and sat down facing her, still intent on my positive-thinking approach. "There's something I forgot to tell you, but Maddie and Jill told me how you took them to New York to see their grandfather's retrospective, and anyway I thought you'd like to know that I went to that same show, too."

"Why?"

"Because my mother took me. We go—"

"Not why did you go, but why would I be interested?" Zenobia said.

"Because I'm your granddaughter, and the paintings were by your husband, who was also my grandfather. Except I didn't know it at the time. But anyway, I think that explains why, when I came here that first night, while you were in the hospital, all the paintings in this house seemed amazingly familiar. Like I'd seen them before. Especially the one over the front door, of the woman walking on the beach. What I really like is the way they're vague, but sort of definite at the same time, but not at all representational."

"Oh, am I to understand that you fancy yourself to be some

kind of an art connoisseur?" said Zenobia, the end of her nose twitching as she spoke.

"Not me. I'm no kind of connoisseur. But my mom is. She knows everything there is to know about art and we go to a lot of shows together and she tells me things, about the pictures and the artists and what materials they used to do what they did. And sometimes if there're other people close by, they stop and listen to her, too."

Zenobia didn't say anything for a couple of minutes, and I was beginning to think that just possibly she might like hearing how my mother really did still know a lot about art. Hah!

"I've been sitting here trying to decide what would possibly be on the walls of that apartment where you live," my grandmother said. "Mickey Mouse? Or maybe teddy bears?"

This time Audrey didn't appear to rescue me. This time, once I could catch my breath, I mumbled something about having to finish a letter to my father, and headed out of the room. As I went, I caught a glimpse of my mother's book, on the floor next to the trash can. Not in it, but leaning against it.

That's the way it went from then on, with Maddie, Jill, and me taking turns. Every day two of us would walk down to the store (for a banana, a container of yogurt, a can of tuna) while the other (lucky one) stayed home for "quality time" with our grandmother. It never really got any better, but after that first time, Jill didn't cry anymore and Maddie didn't break out in hives. On the other hand, at least once during each visit I had with Zenobia, I ended up with the feeling that someone had punched me in the stomach. And I'd bet anything that the others had the same sensation. It's just that we tried not to talk about it much.

In between times the three of us did our best to entertain Zenobia, bringing her the newspaper, the mail, or a glass of juice. We tried to coax her out onto the front porch. ("They've made me a prisoner here, so I might as well stay in," she always said.) Or to watch the news or *Jeopardy!* with us on TV. ("The news is bad and the rest is trash," Zenobia said.)

Other times we cleaned up the kitchen or put the clothes in the washer and dryer or vacuumed the floor—partly to be useful and maybe help Olivia and partly just for something to do. Besides, the more we did around the house, the more time it freed up for Audrey to spend with Zenobia. Which, I guess you might say, was our ulterior motive.

In those little confabs the two aides had on the porch every night, Audrey must have told Ada that our days weren't going too well, because all of a sudden Ada took to entertaining us. She brought jigsaw puzzles from home and videos from the rental store. She tried to teach us to play bridge, which was really fun except that every time it got interesting, Zenobia always managed to thump her cane on the floor and call for a glass of water, a pill, a shawl for her shoulders—or for someone to come and "take this wretched shawl away."

And on the weekends either Elinor or Claire arrived. Somehow my mother hadn't managed to put herself into the rotation yet, and I was beginning to think that she probably never would. I wasn't sure if this made her wimp-of-the-world, or just a whole heap smarter than the rest of us all put together. Part of me knew that if Mom did come, it was sure to be a reenactment of everything that was wrong between her and Zenobia, but the deep-down part of me kept hoping just the same. And whispering *maybe, maybe, maybe.*

Meanwhile, whoever came, Claire or Elinor, would come full of ideas of how things should be done. She would arrive with facts and figures and brochures and flyers about this nursing home and that assisted-living facility, piling them onto our grandmother's bedside table. And it was always only a matter of minutes before Zenobia went after them with her knobby fingers, tearing them into tatters and dropping them on the floor.

Jill, Maddie, and I breathed giant sighs of relief when Sunday afternoon came and the mother or aunt left for home. At least we could all get back to our not-very-satisfactory but predictable weekday life.

And oh, yes. There was one other thing. An unwritten, unspoken rule. Never, not ever, even one single time, would Jill, Maddie, or I have dreamed of complaining to any grownup who came for the weekend. I mean, this had been our idea—and we were sticking with it.

12

Then, almost as if my wanting and not wanting had made it happen, Aunt Claire called in the middle of the following week to say that she wasn't coming for the weekend. That my mother was taking her place.

"Oh, help," I said when Maddie came back from the phone and gave us the message. "What are we going to do?"

The three of us were out on the porch, hoping for a breeze and waiting for the fireflies to appear, and for a few moments we just sat there without saying anything.

"It'll be okay," said Jill. "Your mom's cool, and anyway you've sort of been wanting her to come."

"And sort of *not*, too," I said.

"Well, maybe your dad'll be with her and, you know, sort of defuse things," Jill went on.

"I wish," I said. "I'm going to call him tomorrow, at his office, and see if he's coming. But meanwhile, what do we do about Zenobia?"

"Tell her," said Maddie.

"She'll freak out. She and my mother—it's like World War III waiting to happen. You know if we tell Zenobia she'll just rant and rave."

"Ye-ah," said Maddie, stretching out the word, "but that'll give her a two-day head start for ranting and raving, and by the time Aunt Joyce gets here, maybe things will be okay."

"And maybe not," I said.

"Let's go tell her now," said Jill, jumping up and starting for the door.

It was almost as if Zenobia had been waiting for us, sitting there in her chair and running her fingers down the length of the cane on the table in front of her. "Hmmmph," she snorted. "What's this, the diplomatic corps, here to smooth the way before the invasion?"

"Diplomatic corps?" croaked Jill. "Invasion?"

"Ask the little dark one. She knows what I'm talking about," said Zenobia.

"My mother's coming for the weekend," I said, hoping my voice came out stronger than it felt on the inside.

"I *know* your mother's coming. What do you take me for—a fool? Do you think I don't know what goes on in my own house?"

Zenobia tightened one hand around the top of her cane, and I willed myself not to step backward as I said, "But Aunt Claire just called a few minutes ago to tell us."

"I *know* Claire called. That Ada came in here straightaway, prattling on about how my daughter Joyce would be here on Friday and wasn't that a treat." My grandmother lowered the cane and thumped it sharply on the floor.

"We just—we didn't know that Ada had told you already," said Maddie.

"Well, now you do, so it's mission accomplished," Zenobia said, looking at us one at a time. "Now take yourselves out of here and let me plan how to best entertain my renegade daughter."

When I called my father the next day, he told me that he wasn't coming. "I wanted to, Kiara," he said. "I suggested your mom and I leave Friday morning and stop in the Brandywine Valley for lunch and the Wyeth museum on the way—but she was adamant about this being something she had to do on her own." And if I hadn't known better I'd've thought the "something" was a root canal, or maybe an appendectomy.

Until my mother arrived, Zenobia carried on a silent vigil, which was actually scarier than if she had been whacking and thumping her cane or sweeping things off tabletops. But late on Friday afternoon she came out of her room and had Audrey settle her in a chair just between the living room and the front hall, where she had a clear view of the door.

Once we saw where Zenobia was situated, Jill, Maddie, and I tiptoed through the kitchen and out the back door.

"She's waiting, like a lion ready to pounce," said Maddie. "What do you think she'll do when your mom arrives?"

"I don't know, but I'm going up to the corner to watch for her cab so I can warn her," I said.

But we had no sooner made it around front when a taxi came down the hill and pulled up to the curb. My mother got out and suddenly we were all around her, reaching for her suitcase, her jacket, her tote bag full of books.

"Hi, Aunt Joyce, she's in there waiting—"

"Zenobia's waiting for you—"

"Mom, maybe you should—"

"Girls, I love that you're concerned," my mother said as she headed for the steps. "But it'll be fine. *I'll* be fine. Everything will be fine. Now come in." With that she sailed across the porch and into the house, with the three of us squeezing in the door behind her.

"Well, Joyce," said Zenobia, "you're late."

"Late?" said Mom. "I told Claire to tell you all I'd be here before supper, and I am."

"For the funeral."

"Funeral? What funeral?" asked Mom, and I somehow knew what my grandmother was going to say before my mother figured it out.

"Your father's funeral. I don't seem to remember your being there." Zenobia's words were sharp, and I found myself rubbing my bare arms, as if I were trying to erase the pain she was hoping to cause.

"My father's funeral? You didn't even see fit to tell me until—"

"You could have read it in the *Times*."

99

"I *did* read it in the *Times*. Then I called you and you hung up on me."

"And you didn't come," Zenobia said. "To Lambert's funeral."

The heat in the hall was unbearable, and just when I began to think that the walls were crowding in on us, Audrey came out of the kitchen and helped Zenobia into the living room, muttering, "You people need to go where there's some air." I don't remember the rest of us following them, but somehow we must have, and Maddie, Jill, and I ended up on the piano bench. My mother went to the front window and stood facing out. After a while she sighed and turned around.

"You told me to leave. Never to come again," she said.

"He was your father," said Zenobia, picking at a rough spot on the arm of the chair. "And you didn't come."

My mother shook her head, and when she spoke next the words were slow and careful. "Maybe I was wrong. Maybe I should have come. But it was hard—you don't know how hard—to have my own family—and ever since—all the rest of my life—"

Zenobia's head shot up. "Another wasted opportunity. But you were always good at those, Joyce. Wasted life, wasted talent, wasted—"

"My life was never wasted. My life has been incredibly happy," my mother said, her cheeks suddenly flaming with patches of red. "I have a wonderful husband and a wonderful daughter. And I have my work."

Zenobia made a spitting sound, but before she could say

anything, Mom went on. "How about it, Mother. Can you say the same? Was my father happy? Were you?"

"How *dare* you ask that?" Zenobia shrieked. "Your father was Lambert Jones. And I was his wife." She grabbed a small bowl from a nearby table and threw it against the wall. We all watched, as if in a trance, as splinters of glass showered down.

We were sitting at the breakfast table the next morning when Zenobia came into the room. She had her cane in one hand and stood leaning on it as she said, "Well, Joyce, I'm surprised to see you still here. You're tougher than I would've thought."

"You made me that way," my mother said.

"Hmmmph," said Zenobia. "Well, since you *are* still here, and since you're such an authority on art, I have a job for you today."

As I watched my mother, it was as if a light came on inside her. "Okay," she said. "What do you need me to do?"

"Find a pen, and one of those yellow legal pads, and then I want you to go through the house, the whole house, with the exception of the studio, and write a brief description of every painting you see and its exact location. You may bring it to me at the end of the day."

"But, Zenobia," said Mom, the light suddenly gone from her face, "surely you must already have an inventory. Why would you need me to do that?"

"A job worthy of your talent, my dear," said Zenobia as she turned and thumped her way back to her room.

Strangely enough, while Jill and Maddie and I stood by like

extras in a movie, my mother did as she was told. It was almost as if she had been given a test that she had to pass. All day long she went up and down the stairs, in and out of rooms. And when she was done, she took the written pages into Zenobia's room and handed them to her, without either of them saying anything.

After dinner that night, while Jill and Maddie and Ada played Scrabble in the kitchen, Mom and I went outside. We walked twice around the pine tree at the end of the road and then settled onto the front steps.

"Why am I here?" she said when we had been sitting there awhile. "Why do I care?"

"Because she's your mother," I said.

"I guess. But—come home with me, Kiara. You've done your part here, and when I leave tomorrow, just come with me. The girls will understand. What do you say?"

"I can't."

"Why not?"

"Because she's my grandmother."

My mother put her arm around me and pulled me close, and in the almost-dark I could see her nodding.

Mom left on Sunday afternoon. And once she was gone, once that weekend was over, it was as though all the energy had been sucked out of the house.

13

In all the rest of that Fernhill summer, one murky
weekend in early August really stood out, in a miserable but
good sort of way. The air on Friday had been so heavy and
damp that it was an effort to move, or even to breathe. And
when Aunt Claire arrived late in the afternoon, it was obvious
that she was going to be more Aunt Claire–ish than ever before.

"We've got to get this matter settled," she announced as
Maddie, Jill, and I went over to the car to greet her. "Summer's
skimming along, and this time I've come prepared." She gave us
each a quick kiss on the forehead and headed for the house, calling over her shoulder, "This time we're going to get it *settled*. No
nonsense."

Aunt Claire unpacked her suitcase, washed her face, and
combed her hair—as if getting into battle mode—and then
sailed down the stairs, with the three of us trailing behind her.
By the time we got there, the door to Zenobia's room was open

and she was up from her nap. But if Aunt Claire was in battle mode, then Zenobia was in full body armor.

Jill, Maddie, and I knew it right off, as if there'd been a large red sign over our grandmother's head that said: *I am Zenobia, and if you mess with me today you do it at your own peril.* The three of us stopped at the door, catching hold of the frame. We caught our breath, too, and waited. Aunt Claire, though, was somehow out of tune, or out of sync, or whatever, and she kept going, right into the room, swinging her canvas tote bag up onto the table next to Zenobia and saying, "Now, Mother, I've brought all kinds of new information for you to look at, and we really have to get this taken care of *now.*"

While she was speaking, Aunt Claire was also piling flyers and brochures and booklets onto Zenobia's lap. And no sooner did they land there than my grandmother flicked them off onto the floor, like so many cockroaches.

Aunt Claire tightened her lips into a flat line and dug deeper into the bag, pulling out a video. "And I have this, from Sweet Meadows, out in Carroll County. It's a lovely place with wonderful facilities, and we can all look at the video together—you, me, the girls, and Audrey. We'll—"

With that Zenobia yanked the video away from Aunt Claire, her shaking hands clawing at it, trying to get it open, and finally dropping it onto the floor. "You always were a dull child, Claire," Zenobia said, "but I did think you understood English. Now *get out.* And stay out of this room. I'll let you know if and when I want to see you."

Aunt Claire's face went from pink to red to an even scarier

white. Her mouth moved but at first no words came out, until she finally managed to say, "Joyce was right, all those years ago. She was right when she walked out of here and never came back. And all the while Elinor and I wasted our time trying to please you. But it can't be done, can it?"

Zenobia sighed and put her head back. "Close the door on your way out."

Aunt Claire went out onto the porch, the three of us tagging along after her again. She settled onto the glider, with Maddie next to her, while Jill and I headed for the top step, and we sat down without saying anything. "Has it been like this all summer?" Aunt Claire asked after a while.

I looked at Jill, who looked at Maddie, who looked at me. "She's okay," Jill said, pushing a trail of dust into a pile.

"Yeah, she's okay," I said.

Then we were quiet again till, all of a sudden, like a truck going downhill without any brakes, I felt the words roaring through my head. "Aunt Claire, what happened with my mom and Zenobia?" I blurted out. "I still don't understand. Was there like one big blowup scene, or what? What did my mother do?"

"The only thing Joyce ever did wrong was to inherit her father's talent in art. It started when your mother was a little girl. I mean, when other children were busy tracing their hands, your mother was drawing circus ponies and sea anemones. But my father and Zenobia couldn't just let it alone, leave her be with her colored pencils and pastels. No—she was sent off for art lessons, to classes where she didn't want to be. In the summers Elinor and I went off to sleepaway camp, but your mom was dropped off every morning at the museum for a class in artistic expression. When Elinor and I got baubles and beads for Christmas or our birthdays, Joyce was given a new set of oil paints. And in a *New York Times* article about Lambert Jones, Joyce was described as 'someone worthy to take up her father's mantle.' And she was twelve years old at the time."

Aunt Claire closed her eyes for a moment before going on. "The thing is, by this time your mother hated to draw—hated that she had to keep doing it—but she couldn't stop, and many a time, when she finished something breathtakingly beautiful, she'd turn around and tear it to shreds. And then there was the college thing. While Elinor and I were free to go to regular colleges, your mom was only allowed to apply to art schools and was sent off to Pratt, in New York, to live, as our father decreed, the New York Experience. Only for Joyce, her New York Experience was meeting Warren Birkell during her freshman year."

"But why didn't her mother do something?" I asked. "Why didn't she step in and see—"

"Zenobia could never—would never—stand up to her husband, so she basically sacrificed her daughter for Lambert's sake."

"But when did they stop talking? When did my mom stop coming here and how come Zenobia never came to New York to see her?" My words sounded rushed and choppy, but I had to know.

"It was the year I graduated from college," said Aunt Claire, "and my parents threw a big party and Joyce, who got a ride with a friend who was going to Washington, came down to help celebrate. She also came to tell our parents that she was quitting college and getting married, only she made the mistake of blurting it out right in the middle of the party and ended up creating a major scene."

"What happened?" Maddie asked. "Go on."

"Well, my father was almost apoplectic," Aunt Claire said, running her fingers through her hair. "He screamed and yelled and said he wasn't going to let her ruin her life. He said he forbade it. That he wasn't going to let her give up her art. And by then Joyce is screaming that she hates art, that she'd been forced into it, and it wasn't up to him anymore.

"Then Lambert got into who was this bum anyway and even went so far as to say 'probably someone who wants to latch on to my fame.'"

Aunt Claire paused. "You know, Kiara, your mother was pretty impressive that day. I mean, everyone at the whole party was almost cowering, and there was Joyce telling her father that Warren Birkell didn't need him or anyone; that he was teaching at Columbia and writing a wonderful novel, and that her parents would see for themselves, once they met him. And with that she whipped out a picture of the two of them, Warren with his arm around her, and held it out to Father."

Aunt Claire looked at me, then leaned forward to touch me on the arm. "I don't think it really had anything to do with your dad being black," she went on. "But Lambert was so crazed with anger that he fixated on the race issue and said some dreadful things. Joyce waited it out—just stood there and waited and then she tried one more time, saying that Warren was in New York but he wanted to come down the next day to meet her parents.

"I still remember how Lambert looked, his face red and his hands shaking. He was practically screaming: 'He'll never come in this house!' Then Joyce turned to Zenobia, probably not expecting much help, but she turned anyway, and her mother, my mother, looked her right in the eye and said, 'If you do this to your father, you and this man, you'll never be a part of this family again. And you know I mean it.'"

Jill reached over and took my hand and squeezed it tight while Maddie asked, "And then what happened?"

"Joyce picked up her shoulder bag off that little rocker in the hall and went out the door and down the walk. Elinor and I ran after her, begging her not to go—though we knew deep inside that she had to. I remember Elinor saying, 'If you go now, you know you'll stay gone.' And Joyce said, 'I'm not "going." I'm being *sent*.' And she went, on up the hill and out of sight. And we went back to the house.

"We found out later that because she only had eleven dollars in her wallet and no credit card, Joyce called Warren from the train station and instead of even wiring her the money he came down from New York to pick her up. The next day she withdrew from college, and four days later they were married."

Aunt Claire closed her eyes, and for a while I thought she wasn't going to say any more. Then she sighed and looked right at me. "I've always been ashamed—both Elinor and I have been—of not standing up for Joyce. Of not siding with her. And from time to time, through the years, we tried to keep in touch, but by then your mother didn't want any part of any one of us. And I'm not sure I blame her."

Audrey turned the TV on in the living room and the voices sounded alien and faraway. I stood up and walked down the steps and then back up and sat where I had been before. "I'm glad you told me, Aunt Claire. My mother never did, except a little bit earlier this summer. But you know what? She draws now. All the time. It's like she can't get enough. That's because my dad, a couple of years ago, asked if maybe she would try— just a few sketches—and she did, and then she did more and more, and just this past spring she had a children's picture book come out and it's really, really good, only I showed it to Zenobia and she acted like it was slime."

Aunt Claire put her head back, and when she looked at me again her eyes were red and teary. "I'd like to see your mother's book. And you know something, Kiara, I can't wait to meet your father, the man who gave my sister her gift back."

14

Zenobia stayed in her room with the door closed all weekend. Audrey, or, at night, Ada, would go in carrying trays or doses of medicine, and if Maddie, Jill, and I crept close to the door, we could hear one or the other of them half scolding and half pleading with her. Then, in a matter of minutes, Audrey or Ada would come back out, shaking her head and saying, "She claims she's fixing to stay in there till it suits her to do otherwise, or until hell freezes over. Whichever happens first."

Aunt Claire left late on Sunday afternoon. The rain started in the middle of that night, and by Monday morning it was a pouring-down, soggy, and totally hideous day. The three of us girls were sitting at the kitchen table, eating Jill's special French toast, and I for one was wondering why I was there instead of home in New York living my normal, make-sense life. I'd've bet anything my cousins were thinking the same thing—about Virginia and Pennsylvania.

Out loud, though, we were trying to decide what to do all day, when, for no reason we could figure, it somehow suited Zenobia to come out of her room. We heard her before we saw her, thumping her way along the hall till suddenly she was there, leaning on a counter piled high with baskets and oddly shaped blue bottles and a couple of African masks.

"Hi, Zenobia," said Jill, starting to get up. "Would you like some French toast? I can make some—"

"Why French? Why not Italian or Lithuanian?" Zenobia asked, which is exactly the kind of thing my dad would say, only with him it would've been a joke. "Are you somehow deluded into thinking the French can make toast better than anyone else?"

"Well, I don't—I mean, it's just—" Jill stammered.

"Just one more example of a woeful lack of intellectual curiosity." Zenobia spit the words out as if they tasted bad. She cracked her cane against the chair Maddie had pulled out for her and went over to the refrigerator, peering along one side and then the other in a super-exaggerated way.

"Is she gone? Is she finally out of here?" she asked.

"Who? Is who gone?" I said.

"*Her* mother." Zenobia jabbed a finger at Maddie. "What— did she run out of ways to torture me?"

"That's not fair," said Maddie, her face flaming as red as her hair. "Mom comes all the way over here, and you know she only wants to help. Same as Aunt Elinor and Aunt Joyce do."

111

"One's as bad as the other," my grandmother said, turning to face us. "Just can't wait to put me away someplace. Lock me up in some pee palace and throw away the key."

"That's doubly not fair," said Maddie. "All our mothers want is to find somewhere that you'll be at least sort of happy, and—"

"Hah!"

"You have to go *someplace*," said Jill, "and my mom says you won't even think about going to Virginia or Pennsylvania or even New York, so you could be near to one of your own kids." I could tell by Jill's voice that she was about an inch from crying, but she kept going. "So they do what they can and bring info and brochures and all that stuff for you to look at."

Zenobia's answer to that was a long, slow hiss.

"And besides, they're doing their best. Our moms, I mean," said Maddie. "And you know the doctor said you can't stay on here."

"He's a fool, and *their* best isn't worth much. I certainly don't like what they're coming up with, and even the three of you ought to be bright enough to realize that *they're* not the ones who are going to be imprisoned in one of those places. What's it to them? What do they care if the place smells like urine and is filled with babbling old fools? All they want is to shelve me away and be done with it. Do you understand that, missy? Do you, or you?" said Zenobia, back to poking her finger, at Jill, then Maddie, then me.

Suddenly I heard myself speaking before I knew what I was going to say. "*Then why don't you find your own stinking place?*"

"My point exactly," said Zenobia, though she seemed slightly surprised. "They smell. They stink."

"You *know* what I mean. It's just a word. Get busy and find a place that suits you. *You*—yourself."

Zenobia sat down. "How am I supposed to do that when I'm trapped here, a veritable prisoner?"

"By phone, to start with," I said. "Call a bunch of people, like all those friends who phone and you won't let come over. And the ones who sent the flowers you threw in the trash because you said they smelled like dirty laundry. You have friends, or at least you *did*. Ask them what they know. Then once you've gotten a list together, go ahead and call those places yourself and ask for brochures to be sent right to you. I mean, if you had a computer, we could go on-line and—"

"On-line—off-line," Zenobia snapped. "What do I want with a machine? Anyway, just supposing I did all that, what good would it do me? Only a fool would trust one of those fancy flyers those places send out where they froufrou things up so no one can really tell what they look like. Or smell like either."

"Go see them," put in Maddie. "I mean, first you get the information, and then you go check them out in person."

"On what? My broomstick? I have a perfectly good car, a Checker—like they used for cabs—out in the garage. At least, I guess it's still there, unless they took that, too, when they stole the keys. Claire did that. Stood right next to my bed and said she was taking them."

"Audrey has a car," said Jill.

"And Ada, too," added Maddie.

Suddenly the idea seemed to be growing, right there at the breakfast table. "Yeah," I said. "We can all go and check the places out and see what they really look like."

"Probably *all* smell like urine," said Zenobia, moving her chair a little closer to the table.

"And see if they smell like urine," I said.

"Or Lysol," my grandmother said.

"Or Lysol either," said Jill.

"Then when you find just the right place and get everything all settled and decide what to take with you, you can just go ahead and tell Aunt Claire and Aunt Elinor and my mom that everything's worked out and that you've made your own arrangements," I said in one gulp of air.

"Forget Audrey and Ada. All their cars know how to do is get me to doctor's appointments. Maybe they won't see fit to take me on the rounds to see these places. Maybe they've been brainwashed by the witch-daughters. Maybe—"

"Come on, Zenobia," interrupted Maddie, sounding amazingly like her mother. "Mom and Aunt Elinor and Aunt Joyce may have hired them, but it's *your* money that's paying them. So that makes you in charge, right?"

"It does, doesn't it," said my grandmother, looking from one to the other of us, as if we had suddenly grown brains right in the middle of our foreheads. She pushed her chair away from the table and stood up, thumping her cane three times for emphasis. "This is what I'll need, right away. My address book and a yellow pad from the top desk drawer in my real bedroom, upstairs. Three pencils sharpened to a point. And the phone book, the yellow pages, from that drawer under the back window." With that she made her way back to her room.

The A-team didn't ask what was going on, and we didn't tell. Mostly, I guess, because we wanted to wait and see what would happen, but it was pretty obvious, right from the start, that something *would*.

For the next few days, all anyone could hear from the outside of Zenobia's room was the murmur of her voice as she talked on the phone. Not long after that, things began to arrive. Some by mail, big envelopes and small, filled with flyers and booklets and glossy ads. And we salvaged some from the ones Aunt Claire and Aunt Elinor and Mom had brought. But this time Zenobia read every one.

After reading them she dismissed some, seemingly on a whim, saying, "I just know from looking at the picture of that ugly green carpet that this place smells," or "They're sure to feed a diet of liver and Brussels sprouts in an institution with ponderous furniture like that in the dining room." But, slowly and carefully, she put together a list.

Meanwhile, it was dumb luck or the good fairy or all our combined guardian angels that kept the aunts and mothers from coming to Fernhill on that first weekend after Project Find-Your-Own-Place began. Michael and Steven had some super-important swim meet and desperately needed both Aunt Claire and Uncle Frank to be there. Aunt Elinor was sick with a sinus infection, and my mom and dad went off to the shore for the traditional Birkell family reunion. My mother and the aunts took turns calling to apologize and to ask if we were sure we were all right. And Maddie, Jill, and I took turns reassuring them, without giving anything away.

"Audrey, starting tomorrow, I'll be needing you to drive me to look at some of the places on this list I've compiled," said Zenobia on Tuesday, coming into the kitchen where we girls and Audrey were playing Scrabble. "I've taken my fate into my own hands and have decided that, if I'm to be incarcerated, it will be in a place of my choosing. I'm sure that if we move in a timely fashion we can check out three tomorrow and then possibly finish up on Thursday. Now, I do hope your car is spacious, as I hate to be cramped, and for some reason these three upstarts seem to think they're part of this enterprise."

Audrey looked at Zenobia. She looked at the three of us, and I saw Maddie nod her head just a fraction. Then Audrey looked back at my grandmother. "Well, I don't know, Mrs. Jones. What are your daughters going to say about that?"

Zenobia drew herself up straight and made a sort of spitting noise. She stared at Audrey, and I crossed my fingers until they hurt. *Don't blow it,* I wanted to say. *Please, don't blow it.*

Zenobia opened her mouth, and closed it, then opened it again. "It's not that I need a driver—there are car services or taxis for that—it's just that I need you, Audrey. Because you know about these things, and you'll know what's right and what's slightly off. And what I should demand. Because you're an authority." And I figured right off that that was maybe the only almost-compliment that my grandmother had paid anyone. Ever. "And of course I will compensate you for any travel expenses," she continued. "And bear in mind that the keys to my Checker were stolen by one of those daughters."

Around the table, we all three held our breath until Audrey finally nodded and said, "Tomorrow, then. In the morning, after breakfast."

15

"In the morning, after breakfast" didn't happen as easily as Jill and Maddie and I thought it would. First there was the matter of breakfast itself, which Zenobia didn't want to eat and Audrey said she had to.

"You don't want to be going into those places all weak-kneed and jittery," she said, sliding the tray onto the table next to Zenobia's chair. "If you don't eat something, your concentration won't be much better than a gnat's—and then how're you going to ask all those questions you've got written down?"

"What do you know about my concentration?" my grandmother said, sliding her tray to the very edge of the table.

"Just a little oatmeal, then, to fuel the body."

"I *hate* oatmeal."

"You liked it well enough yesterday," said Audrey. "And the day before that, and the day before—"

"And today I hate it," said Zenobia, crossing her arms over her chest and looking down her long, beaky nose.

"Tea and toast, then, and maybe a little applesauce?"

"Toast," Zenobia said. "No tea, no applesauce, no butter, and absolutely no jam. Toast. And on your way out of here scrape those leeches off the doorframe and take them with you."

The leeches were Maddie, Jill, and me. We'd been hanging around, in and out of Zenobia's room, to make sure it was really going to happen. Her going to check out those places on her first day's list, I mean.

Then, after the breakfast flap, there was the whole clothes thing. Audrey put out a pair of navy blue pants with an elastic waistband, a yellow blouse, and a pair of white canvas lace-up shoes. And Zenobia pitched a fit.

"Old-lady clothes," she sneered. "If I go in anywhere dressed like that they'll think I'm *already* one of the inmates and want to put me back in my cage. First impression is everything, don't any of you know that?" And then she sent the three of us kids upstairs in search of an outfit dredged up out of some distant memory. "I want a proper summer dress, maybe the pink one that buttons down the front, my white high heels, and—yes— bring me my picture hat, with the roses on the brim."

Up in Zenobia's room, we rooted through the closet, peering into garment bags and shoe boxes, peeling back yellowed cleaner's paper and searching behind extra pillows, a folded blanket, and bundles of old checkbooks on the shelf. All the while choking on the musty, dusty, mothbally smell.

"Everything here looks like more of what she has down-stairs, only it's like, you know, winter stuff," said Jill.

"Yeah, but who's going to tell Zenobia?" I asked, and, as if by some prearranged signal, Jill and I both leaned forward to stare at Maddie.

"All right, you guys, so what's the big deal—I'll tell her," said Maddie, turning and leading the way down to the first floor and into our grandmother's room.

"We looked everyplace, and then we looked again," said Maddie, standing in front of Zenobia, but back a bit, out of swatting range. "It's pretty much all winter things up there and not any proper pink summer dresses or picture hats either. So maybe—I mean, do you think you could have given them to the Goodwill or some clothing drive or—"

"Rot," roared Zenobia. "Why would I have done that? Besides, I knew all along those daughters of mine had been helping themselves to things, and now I have proof. If you want my opinion, my pretty summer clothes are walking the streets of Pennsylvania or Virginia, or maybe even New York."

Yeah, right, I thought as I had a sudden mental image of my mother schlepping through the Upper West Side in her jeans and a great swooping picture hat with roses on the brim.

As it turned out, the breakfast and the clothes scenes were mere skirmishes, and the real war was all about the wheelchair. When Zenobia was finally dressed, in her elastic-waist pants, her yellow blouse, and her white canvas lace-up shoes, she made her way shakily down the steps from the front porch. Audrey did a good job of pretending not to hover as she walked beside her, and my cousins and I stood clumped at the bottom, trying not to look and latching on to any prayers we'd ever learned—to keep her from falling. When she was safely down, and as Audrey, Maddie, Jill, and I breathed giant sighs of relief in one big whoosh, Zenobia headed for the car.

"What's that?" she said, peering into the back of Audrey's station wagon and jabbing her finger at the glass. "What—is— that—object?"

"Your wheelchair. I thought it would be—"

"I don't have a wheelchair. Never have and never will."

"Yes, you do, Mrs. Jones," said Audrey.

"Don't tell me what I have. If I can somehow manage to keep track of every painting, every drawing, every piece of sculpture in my house, do you really think I would overlook this loathsome thing? And if you're so smart, where's it been hiding?" said Zenobia, rapping on the glass again.

"In the hall closet," said Audrey. "Right smack in the hall closet."

"And how'd it get there?" asked Zenobia. "Did you bring it? Because if you did, you can just take it right back where it came from."

"Your daughters brought it, that first day, before you came home from the hospital. And it was right nice of them, too, if you ask me. They had in mind that on a pleasant day I might push you around the neighborhood, maybe even down to the shops, but so far you haven't had any inclination to even go as far as the porch."

"My inclinations are my own business," snapped Zenobia. "I should have known it was Claire's doing—and Elinor's, and Joyce's. The sooner they can get me into a contraption like that, the sooner they can lock me away."

Jill poked me in the ribs with a do-something poke, then I nudged Maddie and mouthed, "Say something . . ."

"That's what today is all about," Maddie said, moving closer to our grandmother. "So you can look at a bunch of places, and then once you've seen them you get to pick your own, where you want to be, and then nobody can be putting you where you *don't* want to be, and you'll be in charge."

"Maddie's right," said Audrey, taking hold of Zenobia's arm and steering her to the front of the car.

"Take it out, then," said Zenobia. "Take the chair out."

"Well, the way I see it," said Audrey, opening the door on the passenger side and easing Zenobia into the car, "that chair's not taking up any room we specially need right now, and it's not using up any air we're going to be breathing, so let's just let it be for a while. Besides, some of these places we're visiting are right large, with long halls and grounds you might want to take a look at, and having that chair could come in handy."

"In a pig's eye," hmmmphed Zenobia.

When Audrey pulled up at the front door of Maplecrest, my grandmother refused to get out of the car. "You want these people to think I'm infirm, being dumped out like a sack of potatoes? Just pull over there and park on the lot," she said.

"The girls will be with you," Audrey said. "I'll drop you all off and then catch up."

Zenobia sniffed. "An infirm old sack of potatoes and three tagalongs. No thanks. So just park."

Audrey parked the car and we all made our way slowly across the lot. We were partway up the walk when Zenobia stopped, whacked at a row of Shasta daisies with her cane, and said, "Where's my chair? What do you people think I am, a marathon runner?"

Jill and Maddie ran to the car for the wheelchair, and just as Audrey was trying to help Zenobia into it, my grandmother started in with the cane again, this time aiming at the general vicinity of our ankles. "What are you three staring at?" she yelled as we jumped backward. "Just you wait, you'll be old one of these days. Old and debilitated and discombobulated, and then somebody'll want to put you in a baby carriage and push you around. Just you wait."

"This is not like any baby carriage *I* ever saw," said Audrey, pushing Zenobia around the circular driveway to give her time to calm down. "Not with these nice big wheels to cushion out the bumps and the four of us to give you the ride of your life. No, indeed."

"Shows what you know," said Zenobia.

Inside, Maplecrest was cheerful. So cheerful that it made my skin crawl. There were big bouncy bunches of fake flowers on tables and windowsills. Smiley-face posters beamed from windows and doors, and jingly music rang out around us. And the director, whose name tag said MRS. SULLIVAN, seemed to hippety-hop as she came across the lobby to greet us.

"Oh, Mrs. Jones," she chirped, "we at Maplecrest are so delighted to meet you." *Hop, hop, hop.*

"Why?" said Zenobia.

"A new friend is always a treasure," said Mrs. Sullivan, without missing a beat, or a hop.

"Are you the warden?" Zenobia asked, taking her cane off her lap and clutching it in her right hand, as if she might wield it at any minute.

"Oh, we do love a guest with a sense of humor. I'm Agnes Sullivan, the director here, and I'll be giving you your tour." Then Mrs. Sullivan turned to lead the way down a hall, and as if by some special signal, the music swelled and jingled more than ever.

We walked through the dining room (more bouncy fake flowers and a banner stretched from wall to wall saying WE LOVE AUGUST), the common room, where a group of residents were watching a rerun of *Mister Rogers' Neighborhood*. As we followed the director down another hall, Zenobia reached out and caught the hook of her cane on a doorframe and said, "Stop."

"Is something wrong, Mrs. Jones? Am I going too fast?" said Mrs. Sullivan, her words rippling like a mini-waterfall. "I thought we could go upstairs now and take a look at some of the guest quarters. I think you'll find they're homey and—"

"I won't find they're *anything*, because I'm not going," Zenobia said, looking up at Audrey and jerking her head in the direction of the front door. She then added, "I would, you understand, but if I were to go upstairs I'd be late for my doctor's appointment, and you *know* that wouldn't do. Now, would it?"

We were outside and all the way in the car before Audrey looked at my grandmother and said, "Why'd you fib to that woman like that, Mrs. Jones? You know you don't have any doctor's appointment today."

"Wasn't a fib," Zenobia snapped. "If I'd spent one more minute in that place, I'd've needed not one doctor but a whole passel of them."

The second place on Zenobia's list was Mount Gerard, and it wasn't cheerful at all. The director's name was Mrs. Gossman, and she didn't bounce or chirp, either one. She had a long sort of horse face and her hair hung limply on either side and looked a lot like the faded limp curtains shrouding the windows in the lobby.

"I thought we'd sit and talk awhile," Mrs. Gossman said, pulling her chair close to Zenobia's wheelchair. "And then if you're interested, we could have a little tour."

"Doesn't look like that brochure you sent out," said Zenobia, inching her chair back.

"Well, no," sighed Mrs. Gossman. "But we do our best. Now, I'm sure you have questions, things you want to know about us, and we have things we'll want to know about you."

Zenobia put her head down, staring hard at the carpet.

"You know something," said Audrey, standing up and taking hold of the back of the wheelchair. "We're running a little late today and Mrs. Jones has a doctor's appointment, and we just can't take the chance of being late. So if you'll just excuse us . . ."

The third place was Glen Haven, and when we got there Zenobia wouldn't even get out of the car. "It smells," she said, peering out the open window. "I can tell just by looking at it that it smells. That's the original Pee Palace. Let's just go home."

Audrey started the car without even arguing, and we were barely out of the parking lot when my grandmother's head dropped back and she began to snore. And those little rattly, snuffing sounds were suddenly the saddest thing I'd ever heard.

16

The next day was a repeat performance of the one before. Or, as my father said that Yogi Berra once said, "It was déjà vu all over again."

Zenobia said, "No breakfast." Audrey said, "Yes, breakfast." And after a bit of wrangling they settled on toast again, but this time "with a smidgen—no more, no less—of apricot preserves."

Audrey put out the same navy blue pants with the elastic waist, a striped shirt, and the white canvas lace-up shoes. And Zenobia sent Maddie, Jill, and me upstairs in search of the proper pink dress, the picture hat, and the white high heels. Which we didn't even bother to look for. Instead, we sat on the edge of the window seat counting out the time till we could go back down.

"Hmmmph," snorted Zenobia when we showed up empty-handed. "Remind me to inform those daughters of mine that I want my clothes back. Once they've been properly cleaned, of course."

When Zenobia, in her navy blue pants, striped shirt, canvas shoes, and an Orioles cap from I-haven't-a-clue-where, finally made it to the car, she settled into the front seat without a murmur. But as soon as Audrey started the ignition, Zenobia began to pull and tug at the seat belt.

"What's the matter, Mrs. Jones? Did we forget something?" asked Audrey, cutting the engine.

"I need to get out of this car," my grandmother snapped. "I need to get out and go around and see if that confounded chair is still in back." She let go of the seat belt and turned to fumble with the door handle.

"Sure it's back there," Audrey said. "And like I said yesterday, it's not taking up any space we're in desperate need of, and if you direct me to go around there and take that chair out and tote it back into the house—why, all that would make us late for your appointment with Mr. Prem at the Blackstone."

"Is that the truth?" asked Zenobia, slitting her eyes to look at Audrey and then over her shoulder at the three of us.

"The gospel truth," said Audrey, nodding.

"I dislike tardiness," said Zenobia, folding her hands in her lap. "And rank it right up there with the seven deadly sins. So you may proceed."

And, of course, once we got there, my grandmother, her cane resting on her legs, rode up the walkway to the Blackstone in her wheelchair, with Maddie and me pushing and Jill and Audrey walking just behind.

128

The inside of the Blackstone was so incredibly normal. The furniture in the waiting area looked like stuff that people would really sit on, and not like something swiped from a funeral parlor. There were no bouncy bunches of fake flowers and no smiley faces peering out at us from the corners. No treacly music oozed around us, and instead we could hear the sound of ringing telephones and the sort of cheerful rumble of a copying machine.

The walls, a yellow-almost-gold color, were splotched here and there with framed posters from a bunch of different art museums—the Barnes Foundation, the National Gallery, the Metropolitan, and the Whitney. A receptionist in a red dress sat at a desk in the middle of the floor, and when she got up and came toward us she walked instead of hopping, and when she spoke she didn't chirp.

"Good morning," she said. "Mrs. Jones?"

And all of us (except Zenobia) nodded at once.

"Mr. Prem is looking forward to meeting you, and if you'll just follow me, I'll take you to his office."

Mr. Prem was not very tall and not very much of anything, and if you saw him waiting for a bus or something you might not even notice him. But then he smiled. And spoke in a voice that was way bigger than he was. And held out his hand to Zenobia, saying, "Mrs. Jones, I'm happy to meet you. And I see you've brought your entourage."

And for the first time in two days, Zenobia saw fit to introduce the rest of us. After a fashion, anyway.

"How do you do, Mr. Prem. This is Audrey. She takes care of me. The others are my granddaughters. The redhead is Maddie, bossy like her mother. The dark one is Kiara, and she's late on the scene and from New York. That last one is Jill, bland as pudding—but sometimes she surprises me."

"I'm glad the four of you came along," said Mr. Prem, pushing Zenobia's wheelchair over to a table set in a bay window and motioning the rest of us to sit down. "I know Mrs. Jones will have questions, and I'm sure you will, too."

Mr. Prem took his place on the other side of the table and waited in a comfortable way, as if it were the most normal thing in the world for the six of us to be sitting there without saying anything. Jill kicked me under the table, and I kicked Maddie and was about to blurt out some meaningless blather just to fill the space when Zenobia leaned forward and said, "The cat. What about the cat?"

"Ah, yes, the cat," said Mr. Prem. "And his name is?"

"He is called Eleven," said Zenobia. "No more, no less. I've found, through the years, that by numbering them, I've left my cats free to evolve into the animals they were meant to be. Now: is there a provision for cats?"

"There could be," said Mr. Prem. "But it would mean some concessions on Eleven's part. Our caretaker, Mr. Rhea, lives on the property and has been known to take on our clients' pets from time to time—right now he has three cats and a pug dog in residence. You could visit if you wanted."

"Or," said Zenobia, "I suppose he could stay at Fernhill— my late husband's house. It's to be bequeathed to the Art Institute, you know, and Eleven could readily become a part of the arrangement."

"Whatever you decide," said Mr. Prem. "But I'd be happy to introduce you to Mr. Rhea so you could see if you thought he and the cat would be a good match."

Then we were back to the silence again. But not for long, because all of a sudden Zenobia took charge. She asked about the cost, and what she would be allowed to bring with her. And what she wouldn't. She asked about having her hair done and getting to doctor's appointments and if she would have access to a library. She asked if the rooms were bright and airy and if the food was edible.

"I think you'll find our food more than edible—it's very good," said Mr. Prem. "In fact, I'd like to suggest that the five of you come back and have a meal with us sometime and see for yourselves. There's plenty of variety and—"

"I'll have one now," Zenobia said. "We'll *all* have one now."

"Well, er . . ." Mr. Prem hesitated.

"You have food, don't you?" Zenobia asked. "It's almost lunchtime, and I generally eat lunch. Especially when you consider that all I was given for breakfast was a little toast."

"Yes, of course, but it's just that dinner is our more formal meal, and I thought you might enjoy that more," said Mr. Prem.

"What's the matter?" snapped Zenobia. "Do you hide the old people at dinnertime?"

Mr. Prem stood up and held out his hand. "Lunch it is, Mrs. Jones. Lunch it is."

I don't know how Mr. Prem did it, but by the time we got to the dining room, there was a table ready for us. And the food *was* good. Especially the brownie with ice cream on top.

After lunch Zenobia, Audrey, and Mr. Prem sat drinking tea while Jill, Maddie, and I checked out the other people in the room. Even though there were a bunch of wheelchairs and walkers and canes leaning every which way, everyone looked pretty regular except for a couple of men who seemed to be asleep and a woman in a yellow dress catching butterflies where there were no butterflies.

I was sort of spacing out, wondering whether Zenobia would end up eating with any of these people, and if so, which ones. Or if she'd lay claim to a table in the corner by herself. I had just mentally seated her with a man and a woman at the far end of the room when I heard my grandmother say, "I'll take one."

"Tea? You'd like more tea?" asked Mr. Prem, beckoning to a server.

"One unit. Or apartment. Or cell. Or whatever you call your accommodations here," said Zenobia. "I'll take one, preferably with that den you spoke of, as I have these daughters who descend from time to time and I need space for them—or for me to escape to."

"Now, Mrs. Jones, you haven't even *seen* a unit yet," said Audrey, leaning close, then jumping back when Zenobia swatted at her.

"Mrs. Jones," said Mr. Prem, "we'd be thrilled to have you,

but I'm sure you'll want to talk this over with your daughters. It's a big decision and—"

"I *know* it's a big decision," my grandmother flared. "And one they've been trying to make for me for weeks. I am, however, capable of making my own choices. And if it's money you're worried about, contact my attorney, Henry Taylor at Taylor, Taylor, and Smith. He'll come by here and sign what needs to be signed—and what he can't sign, he'll bring to me to sign. Is that clear enough?"

"Perfectly," said Mr. Prem. "And it just happens that we do have a vacancy with a den."

"And just how does there happen to be a vacancy?" Zenobia asked, pushing her empty teacup across the table. "Don't people like it here?"

"Mr. Corcoran," said Mr. Prem. "It was his unit."

"And he . . . ?" prodded Zenobia.

All of a sudden I was crossing my fingers under the table and willing Mr. Prem not to blow it by telling her Mr. Corcoran had moved to Florida or Nova Scotia or to live with his daughter in Kansas.

"He died," said Mr. Prem with a sigh. "He died."

"Hmmmmmph," said Zenobia. "I guess you get a lot of that here." And she propelled her wheelchair over to the far wall, where she reached out and straightened a Monet print with the tip of her cane.

17

All the way home in the car Zenobia dictated lists, though none of us had a pencil to write with, or even any paper.

"The Morris chair—don't forget that," she said. "And my own pillows—theirs are sure to be lumpy. And books—books—books—and while you're at it, make a note for me to track down my copies of *The Great Gatsby* and *House of Mirth*. They were missing last time I checked, and that Elinor always has been one to walk away with books. And then start a list of things not to be taken under any circumstances—planters, no matter what kind, and anemic-looking African violets, and that photograph of my father sitting on a pony that, for some reason, people seem to think I should be fond of."

Zenobia kept this up the whole way home, and when we pulled up in front of Fernhill, she turned and glared at each one of us, her eyes boring right through to our innards. "I can see that I'm going to have to tend to most of this myself, since not one of you saw fit to come prepared."

"Yikes. How were we supposed to know she was going to decide right on the spot and want to make *lists* then and there?" said Maddie later on, when the three of us were in the kitchen helping Audrey fix supper.

"And then to give us the evil eye like that," said Jill. "On account of we didn't see fit to *come prepared*."

"Yeah, and all the while I had this creepy feeling that she was going to snap her fingers and turn us into snakes or toads or something," I put in, reaching into the refrigerator for salad stuff.

"Don't you fret, any one of you. Just let Mrs. Jones catch her breath. Before you know it, she'll be making more lists and plans up one side and down the other," said Audrey, sliding a tray of veggie burgers into the oven.

But Audrey was wrong. Way wrong.

"She's slumped over in her chair and drumming her fingers against the table edge and not saying anything, even when I told her that Audrey had fixed her favorite kind of chicken because we knew she didn't like veggie burgers like the rest of us were having," said Jill, coming back from taking Zenobia her tray. "I mean, she didn't even fuss and ask what made me think she even *liked* chicken? And what she really wanted was lamb stew or salmon cakes or something. It was eerie."

"I told you girls your grandmother's worn out—not just body worn out but up here, too," said Audrey, tapping her head with her blue-speckled fingernails. "Just you keep in mind, she made a big decision today, and I expect she's got a lot to think about tonight."

"Do you think she'll change her mind and decide not to go?" I asked, dumping ketchup and pickle relish on my burger.

"From what I know about Mrs. Jones, I don't think she's much for mind-changing," said Audrey. "But that doesn't make it any easier. Let's give her some time, and then I'll go and check on her."

After we finished eating, Audrey did go check on Zenobia. She was gone pretty long, till way after the cat was fed and the dishes done and the counters wiped down. When she came back carrying the supper tray, there was the chicken and applesauce and peas sitting untouched on the plate and looking only a little more tired than when Jill took it in.

That night, after Ada came and Audrey left, we watched TV in the living room, and not once, even when the commercials boomed out, was there any cane-thumping or whacking from Zenobia's room. No angry voice saying to *turn that thing off*.

Zenobia's mood or state or slump lasted well into the next day. The door to her room was kept closed, and it seemed to vibrate with the silence coming from inside. Food trays were sent back almost untouched, and there were no demands for juice or tea or Mint Milano cookies, which, I guess because of the way we'd added them to the store lists all summer, our grandmother had taken a liking to.

It didn't take long for Maddie, Jill, and me to figure out that

Zenobia dormant was way scarier than Zenobia erupting like Mount Vesuvius. The three of us crept around the house, not quite sure what to do and never once thinking about whose turn it was to escape to the store.

"Maybe we shouldn't have," I said when we had finally settled onto the front porch after lunch. "Talked her into making her own decision, I mean. Convinced her to find her own place. Maybe we should've just let her go on tearing up all those flyers and brochures our mothers brought down."

"Yeah," said Jill, pushing her feet against the floor so that the glider made a screechy noise. "Maybe we should've. And maybe we shouldn't have dragged her around to look at those places."

"Aw, come on, you guys," broke in Maddie. "You know darn well that not one of us could convince Zenobia to do what she didn't want to do. Or go where she didn't want to go, either. Besides, it's obvious to everybody that she can't stay in this house. Mom said the doctor said her Parkinson's is getting worse. Now let's *do* something. Anybody want to play Scrabble?"

Jill and I didn't answer, and we just sat there listening to the screech of the glider and the squawk of some truly annoying bird up in the maple tree.

"Can't you stop that thing from squeaking?" snapped Maddie after a while.

"It's a *bird*," said Jill. "What do you want me to do— *shoot* it?"

"Not the *bird*—the glider," I said. "Just stop pushing it with your feet."

"Well, pardon the heck out of me," said Jill, giving an extra-hard push.

Our words hung there in the hot August air and seemed to be getting louder and louder. "Oh, no," I said, putting my head in my hands. "We sound like Zenobia. Three Zenobias in training."

"We can't," wailed Jill. "We won't. Let's make a pact right now that it'll never happen. That we won't let it."

"The anti-Zenobia pact," said Maddie.

"Yeah," I sighed. "But meanwhile, she's still not eating, or talking, or doing much of anything."

"Audrey's watching her," Maddie said, getting up and heading for the door. "She says if Zenobia's not back to normal by tomorrow she's calling the doctor. And I'm getting the Scrabble board unless somebody has a better idea."

Late that afternoon, a silvery gray car pulled up in front of the house. A tall man with wispy blond hair and a worn-looking briefcase got out and came up the steps to the porch where the three of us were sitting on the floor around the Scrabble board, not playing anymore but too listless to actually put the game away.

"Good afternoon, young ladies," he said. "You must be Zenobia Jones's granddaughters. I'm Henry Taylor, your grandmother's lawyer, and she called me this morning and asked me to stop out. We have some business to take care of."

"She called you?" I asked, without quite meaning to. "Today?"

"Yes, indeed. This morning, almost as soon as I got to the office. But if Mrs. Jones is resting, I can wait."

"No, that's okay," said Maddie. "I'll get Audrey. She's the aide."

"So, any good words," said Mr. Taylor, looking down at our game and the jumble of letters.

"We gave up," said Jill. "It's too hot and the tiles kept sticking to our fingers."

I had just given Jill a weird *sticking to our fingers?* kind of look when Audrey opened the screen door and came out. "Yes, hello, Mr. Taylor. Mrs. Jones is waiting for you."

"What's going on?" asked Jill, once Mr. Taylor had followed Audrey into the house.

"Well, Zenobia said there'd be stuff to sign, about moving to the Blackstone and all," I said, scooping up tiles and dumping them into a tattered brown paper bag.

"So you think she's really going to go?"

"You heard Audrey," Maddie said, coming back out onto the porch. "She said our grandmother's not one to change her mind. Hey, and here's a flash—just now, when I was coming by her room, I heard a thump, as in a cane thump, and Zenobia's voice telling Mr. Taylor not to be a dolt—just to do as he was told."

Somehow this seemed to cheer us and we cleaned up the rest of the game, went into the house in search of lemonade, set the table for supper, got our clothes out of the dryer and sorted them and put them away on the third floor, and were back on the porch when the lawyer came out. Almost an hour later.

"Well, goodbye, ladies," he said. "Have a good rest of the

summer. And by the by, your grandmother wants to see the three of you in her room right now."

Zenobia was sitting in the Morris chair, her cane across her knees, her black eyes flashing. "Well," she said. "I've done my part—the hard part—and now I want you to get your mothers here next Friday. No excuses. And let *them* do something for a change. There's packing to be done. And sorting. Things to be disposed of. Next Friday, do you understand? And no shilly-shallying."

18

By five-thirty the following Friday afternoon Aunt Elinor and Uncle Ben, Aunt Claire and Uncle Frank, and the twins, Michael and Steven, were all at Fernhill. We were crowded into the living room, where Uncle Frank was trying to take a vote between pizza and carryout Chinese food, except that people kept changing their minds.

"How about pizza for the kids and Chinese for the grownups?" said Uncle Ben, taking out paper and pencil.

"But I want *Chinese*," said Jill. "We've had pizza a bunch of times, but I haven't had a spring roll practically all summer."

"And I actually have a yen for pizza," said Aunt Claire. "Besides, we don't know whether Joyce will be arriving before or after supper, or what she'll want once she gets here."

"Okay," said Uncle Frank. "*Some* pizza, and *some* Chinese. Now, I'll give you a couple of minutes and then I'm taking another and final vote—so pick one. And we'll get extra of both for Joyce."

"But what *kind* of pizza?" asked Michael. "We like tons of pepperoni but not yucky peppers or broccoli or stuff."

"And what kind of Chinese?" asked Maddie. "I mean, with shrimp, because if there's shrimp, then that's what—"

"No wonder you can't decide what to do with *me*—you people can't even decide what to eat for *dinner*," said Zenobia, suddenly appearing in the doorway.

"Mother!" said Aunt Claire, turning around. "I knocked on your door when we got in, but I guess you were sleeping and didn't hear me."

"I heard you," said Zenobia. "And I must say, Claire, that even your knock is imperious."

Before anyone could think of what to say next, Zenobia looked out over the crowd, sniffed, and said, "Well, I see that Joyce isn't here. I'm not surprised."

"My mom is coming," I said. "She said late this afternoon— maybe the train was late or—"

"Hmmmmmph. Well, when she does, and when you've all figured out *what* to eat and have *finished* eating it, you may let me know. I have things to say." And with that Zenobia made her way back to her room, thumping her cane on the floor as she went.

Somehow, between the two of them, Uncle Ben and Uncle Frank managed to get the orders sorted out and left to pick up the food. The twins were watching a ball game on TV, Maddie and Jill were setting the table, and the aunts were in the kitchen talking to Audrey while she fixed Zenobia's supper. And I escaped to the front porch to watch for my mother's cab.

I hate waiting and watching for things, hate that time-warp feeling of staring at the place where something is supposed to happen till finally a kind of numbness sets in. I was just at that point, my eyes glued to the top of the street, when a car swung around the corner. At first I thought it was the uncles, back with the food, till suddenly it morphed into my parents' red Honda Accord, and I was down the steps, racing toward the car as soon as it stopped.

"That's what I call a greeting," said my father, laughing as he got out of the car.

"You're *here*," I yelled. "You're *both* here, and now Dad can get to meet Jill and Maddie and the rest. And Zenobia. Come *on*. You can get your stuff later."

I caught hold of my mother with one hand and my father with the other and dragged them up the steps, across the porch, and into the house. And suddenly the hall was filled with people: Aunt Claire and Aunt Elinor, Audrey, Jill, Maddie, and even the twins. And then the uncles piled in behind us, the smell of pizza and Chinese food floating over the top of us all. Then there were handshakes, and hugs, and those grownup air kisses, till Mom broke away, saying, "I want to take Warren down to meet Zenobia."

"Good luck," said Aunt Claire. "She appeared a while ago and let it be known that she'd see everyone *after* dinner, and would have something to say at that time."

Right away my mother stepped back, as if a giant insect had

come down and stung her. "If that's what she said—then—well, okay. We'll wait."

"Why don't we just give it a try?" said my father. "Knock on the door and—"

"No, Warren. No. Please. You don't understand," my mother said.

Dad looked like he had a whole bunch more to say, but he stopped himself just as Mom put her hand on his arm, as if to hold him back. "Please," she said again. "If Zenobia said . . . We'll see her later."

My father looked from Aunt Claire to Mom to me. He shrugged and said, "Later it is, then."

After dinner, and after Zenobia's tray was collected and the dishes were done, and Ada had come and Audrey had gone, our grandmother made her appearance. She thumped her way through the dining room, pausing to tap the chair at the head of the table with her cane and nod for Uncle Ben to carry it into the living room. Once it was there, in the exact spot that suited her, Zenobia settled into it, resting her cane across her lap and looking around. "And *you*," she said, nodding at my father, who was standing next to the couch, "must be Warren Birkell."

"Yes," said Dad, starting forward, his hand held out. "We finally meet."

"Well, as you can plainly see," said Zenobia, turning away, "dealing with this family is much like herding cats. All of you, *sit down*."

"Now, Mother, what—"

144

"Claire, is it impossible for you to follow even the simplest directions? Now, sit." Zenobia fingered her cane, as if at any minute she might physically send Aunt Claire into the closest chair. "And turn that infernal television *off.*"

There was a general scrambling for seats: the grownups on the furniture and Jill, Maddie, and me lined up on the floor under the windows. Michael and Steven tried to squish themselves into a wicker rocker, all the while lurching backward and forward until Uncle Frank caught one of them by the shoulders and planted him firmly on the piano bench.

"Now," said Zenobia, when we were more or less settled, "I am going to say what I have to say just once, so you'd best pay attention."

"What is it . . ."

"We came as soon . . ."

Zenobia glowered and waited till Aunt Claire's and Aunt Elinor's half-sentences faded away. "I have made my decision," she said. "And I have made my plans, so you'd best listen carefully. In very short order I will be moving to the Blackstone."

"Oh, that's wonderful," said Aunt Elinor. "The brochure was lovely, and I thought you'd—"

"Fool!" snapped Zenobia.

"From all I hear—" broke in Aunt Claire.

"I'm so glad you've—" began my mother.

"I certainly hope that none of you have the mistaken idea that my decision has anything to do with what you did or didn't do." Zenobia had suddenly become an equal-opportunity glarer and took the time to scowl at one grownup and then the next, all the way around the room. "If anything, it's the upstarts that did it. So you may blame or thank them, as the case may be."

"But, Zenobia, that's good news," said Uncle Ben, leaning forward and rubbing his hands together.

"And how about the arrangements?" asked Aunt Claire.

"Have you worked out the finances?" said Aunt Elinor.

"There'll be a lot to take care of—so many details," my mother added.

Zenobia drew herself up in her chair. "The arrangements are made—any questions may be directed to Mr. Prem at the Blackstone. The finances are seen to, thanks to my attorney, Mr. Taylor. And you should know by now—I've said it often enough—that this house and its contents will go to the Art Institute. Your father set up a trust that will provide for me. So don't waste your time slavering over a will and trust that cannot be broken."

"But, Mother," said Aunt Claire, "we don't *want* your money—and we've known about the Art Institute for years. We just want to be sure you're content."

"Hmmmph," said Zenobia. "And, Joyce, you made the brilliant observation that there will be a lot to take care of. That's where you all come in. In the next two days, I want things— taken care of. Lists made, the belongings I'll be taking set aside, and all that ticky-tacky refuse in bureau drawers gotten rid of. There's a dump somewhere—find it and put those big cars you all insist on driving to good use. Now, are there any questions?"

"Which paintings are you going to take?" asked Maddie, scrunching forward, closer to Zenobia.

"None," our grandmother said. "That was one life and this is another. The old is finished."

"*No,*" I cried, suddenly finding myself across the room, in front of Zenobia. "That *was* your life and this *is* your life and you can't have one without the other because they're all tangled and overlapping and jumbled into who you *are.*"

There was a weird stillness in the room until Zenobia looked over at me and said, "Three."

"Three what?" asked Aunt Elinor.

"You always were a little dim, Elinor," said Zenobia. "Three *paintings*. I'll take three paintings. And let the leeches pick them—let them do something for eating my food all summer, and sleeping under my roof."

Jill, Maddie, and I looked at each other, then at Zenobia, not quite sure what to say. Then Jill slid over next to me, leaning close to our grandmother and saying, "My mother's not dim, Zenobia. And you know it."

Zenobia looked down at her, the corners of her mouth twitching. "No, I know it," she said. "And you're not so much like pudding after all, are you?"

Jill kept staring, for what seemed like hours, until Zenobia sighed and said, "No, your mother's not dim."

Dad caught up with Zenobia as she was making her way out of the room. "Mrs. Jones—Zenobia, if you don't mind—I'd like to talk to you for a while," he said.

"There's nothing to say," answered my grandmother, starting down the hall to her room.

"I think there's a great deal to say."

"I read your books and I liked them."

"Hang the books," said Dad, his voice rising briefly. "You are, for better or worse, my wife's mother and my daughter's grandmother, and it's time we got to know each other. Either now, or tomorrow morning."

Zenobia stopped. She stood for a stretched-out while without turning around. Finally she said, "As you see fit."

My father looped one arm around my mother's shoulders and one arm around mine, and together the three of us followed Zenobia into her room.

19

Leave the door open, Kiara," said Dad as we went into Zenobia's room. "There's nothing in this conversation that's private. In fact, I hope the others will join us."

"I don't seem to recall inviting the world in here," Zenobia snapped as she settled into her chair. But she didn't tell me to close the door, and so it stayed open, with sounds from the television and bits of conversations throughout the house drifting in from time to time. She rested her cane across her lap and waited while Mom and Dad pulled two straight chairs from across the room and I planted myself on the floor in front of the bed, where I'd be able to watch the three of them.

"Well?" she said. "You called this meeting, I believe."

"Not a meeting. Not at all," my father said. "As I just told you, I think it's time, after seventeen years, that we got to know each other. I love your daughter. Her background, her family, the rift between you, are all parts of who she is—parts I'd like to be able to share."

"Hmmmph," sniffed Zenobia. "I'm sure she's had a great deal to say on *that* subject."

"No, actually," said Dad. "We've talked about what happened very little. Hardly at all."

"She walked out of this house," my grandmother said.

"Mother, you *know* that's not the whole story!" My own mother's voice was high and quivery. "I walked out because you and my father told me that if I married Warren I would never be welcome here again."

I watched my father as he leaned forward, his skin glowing like well-polished wood under the light. "Because I was a black man?" he asked.

"Because you were *any* man," said Zenobia, turning to look at him. "My daughter had a talent—and she failed to honor it."

"No," said Dad, shaking his head. "Joyce has honored that talent many times over. In the way she's raised our daughter. In the work she did at the bookstore. In the one book that's already out and the two she's working on now. Wonderful, glorious pictures."

Zenobia's eyes flicked over to the copy of my mom's book, which now rested on the windowsill, and I knew, more than anything, that there were sneery, spiteful words about bears and picture books that she was dying to say. But before she could let them spill out, my father went on.

"And anyway, in the end, wasn't it up to Joyce? I chose my way in life—my parents raised me to know I had that right—

just as Kiara will choose hers. And I tell you, Zenobia"—my father locked his fingers and bent his hands out backward till the knuckles cracked—"there's nothing she could do that would banish her from my life."

All of a sudden it seemed as if my mom and I weren't there. That it was only my father and my grandmother in the room.

"You say that now," said Zenobia.

"And mean it forever," said Dad. "No argument, no fight, no words, no action could make me turn against my child. My mother and father, my sisters and brothers—well, we don't always like each other every minute of every day—but we do love each other." He shrugged and went on, "And family is family."

"In *your* family, perhaps," said Zenobia, wrapping her fingers around her cane. "I generally make it a practice never to explain myself, so I will only say that my life was devoted to Lambert Jones—and his art. Our children were to fall into place, without any undue mollycoddling."

"That's a little hard on the kids, isn't it?" asked my father as he turned to wink at me.

"I don't see why." Zenobia stiffened her back and drew herself up in her chair. "I was reared that way and without any apparent damage."

Right, Zenobia, I thought, swallowing down a giant laugh. *Right, right, right.* After that, it took all my strength to keep from jumping up and running across the room. To keep from yelling out, *Maybe that's why you're the way you are. Maybe because of something that happened a long time ago. But what was it . . . and when . . . and why?*

"But, Zenobia," my mother cried out, suddenly finding her voice, "you never told us anything about your upbringing. Never *would* tell us."

Zenobia's face was rigid, and her words came out like pieces of chipped ice. "Let's just say it was adequate. And leave it at that."

The room was quiet. I stared down at the squiggly pattern in the rug for what seemed to be hours, and when I looked up, Aunt Claire and Aunt Elinor were standing just inside the door, with Jill and Maddie in front of them.

My cousins scooted over to sit next to me, but other than that, the stillness hung over the room. I had just about decided that we were all frozen like that forever, when Aunt Claire and Aunt Elinor pushed themselves away from the wall and went over to my mother.

"Joyce, I'm sorry," they said at the same time.

"We should have stood up to—stood up for you," said one of the aunts.

"We should have done more to keep in touch," said the other.

By then I had a giant lump in my throat and thought maybe I was listening to something I shouldn't have been listening to. But still, Maddie and Jill and I inched forward so we could hear.

"You tried some—and I—besides, it was complicated," said my mom. "And I always *knew*—I was *sure*—that if I'd been in your shoes I'd've reacted just the way you did. Because I knew firsthand what it was like to stand up to Zenobia."

With that, my grandmother brought her cane down hard, hitting the edge of a metal trash can. "If this maudlin reconciliation scene is over—are we through here?" She turned to look at my father and said, "And don't think, because we've had this little chat, that you've wormed your way into the will."

Dad went over to Zenobia's nightstand. He poured a glass of water and handed it to her, smiling. "I don't want anything from your will, Zenobia. None of us do. But since I'm a little late to the party, as it were, I'm curious about the paintings and the house and the Art Institute. Will Lambert Jones's work stay here? In this house?"

Zenobia drank her water all the way down. She sighed and closed her eyes for a moment. "Lambert decided many years ago that everything would go to the Art Institute downtown. He was on the faculty there for a while. They will make all the decisions about selling the paintings—museums have been clamoring for them for years. Of course, they'll keep some in their own gallery, but not in this house. Not if I'm not here to watch over them."

Zenobia's face suddenly seemed to glow, in a way I'd never seen it before. As if, at last, she was talking about something really important. "And as for Fernhill, the plans are for it to be a study center, and also available for artists-in-residence at the institute. And Lambert's studio will stay the way it's always been."

At the mention of the studio my head jerked up, and for one wild and crazy moment I was sure that my grandmother was going to reach out and tap me on the shoulder and say, "Before I leave Fernhill, I want Kiara to see the place where her grandfather, the grandfather she never knew, did his work." But Zenobia still had that same spacey look on her face, and after a bit she leaned back in her chair and closed her eyes again. "And now I'm tired," she said.

20

I'm not quite sure what I expected the next day—maybe that everything would be changed. But it didn't happen that way, and the rest of the weekend went exactly as Zenobia had ordered. It was as though she had written the script and all of us were just following along, reading our parts and coming in on cue.

We made lists. We assembled the things Zenobia was taking to the Blackstone. We threw stuff away. And more stuff, and more and more. Bureau drawers were dumped out, and boxes pulled off shelves and from under beds. Funky-looking clothes were dragged out of closets and draped over chairs and banisters. Tattered purses and black and green and red pointy-toed shoes lined the second-floor hall, and stacks of catalogs and old *National Geographic*s grew on the landings.

In the beginning my mother and her sisters stopped and exclaimed over everything, and they sounded more like sisters than they had all summer. They oohed and ahhed, and played the *Do you remember?* game. They argued about who had worn what and where the jewelry box with the dancing ballerina had come from. Uncle Frank pointed out that at the rate they were going it would take seventeen weekends to go through everything—and that Zenobia had given them *one*.

From then on we all became reckless, hardly looking as we filled giant leaf bags with old school notes, autograph books, warped tennis rackets, and boxes of jigsaw puzzles. We tied the top of each bag and lugged it out onto the porch—and went back to start on another drawer or cupboard.

Meanwhile, the uncles and my father made trips to various stores for empty cardboard boxes, more leaf bags, and carryout food.

Sometimes Zenobia would emerge from her room to whack her cane against the newel post in the first-floor hall, waiting for one of us to come bouncing a bag of trash down the steps, heading for the porch. "Everything personal must go. I won't have strangers pawing through the remnants of our lives," she would say, in broken-record mode. "I hope I don't need to remind you to touch *nothing* belonging to the institute. And the basement is off-limits to you all. I have the key to Lambert's studio, and I intend to hand it over to the appropriate person—at the appropriate time."

Zenobia was going through this routine on Saturday afternoon when Mom and I happened to be clomping down the stairs with what had to be our seventy millionth bag, and my father was coming in the door with a twelve-pack of Cokes and a bag from Starbucks.

"About the studio, Zenobia," said my mother, dropping her bag and letting it slide the rest of the way down. "I know Kiara would really love to see it, and since she never knew her grandfather, and now that Warren's here, I'd like to take them both down to see it. If it's okay."

"It's not," snorted Zenobia, heading back to her room and pausing only long enough to turn and say, "And that's a regret they will have to live with."

My mother turned that same spooky greenish-white she had the day I first asked her about her family, and just seeing her that way made something deep inside me hurt.

"Why is she so *mean*?" I whispered. My father shook his head and somehow managed to hand me the Cokes and the Starbucks bag, pull my mother close, and kiss her on the forehead—all at the same time.

The next morning Uncle Ben, Uncle Frank, and Dad began loading bags into their cars for their first trip to the dump. Aunt Claire, Aunt Elinor, and my mother started in on the linen closet, sorting worn bath towels, lumpy pillows, and yellowish dresser scarves that had once been white. Their pace didn't seem as frantic as the day before, and as soon as we were sure they were all totally involved in conversation, Maddie, Jill, and I snuck off to select the pictures for Zenobia to take to the Blackstone.

"Let's start on the first floor and work our way up and then down again," said Maddie.

"Okay," I said. "Except I already know."

"You already *know*?" said Jill. "It was only on Friday night Zenobia said we could each choose a painting—"

"Actually she said *the leeches* could pick the paintings," said Maddie, rolling her eyes.

"Well, yeah," said Jill. "Anyway, that was Friday, and as far as I'm concerned, yesterday there wasn't even time to *think*, and here it is today—and you already *know*?"

"I've known since the first night I was here," I said. "I mean, known which was my favorite, and I figured we'd each want her to take our favorite, and that way when we come to visit we can look at it."

"Yeah, okay. So which is it?" said Jill.

"The one over the front door with the woman walking on the beach and the rocks sticking out and it's sort of real and sort of not. And I've always hoped the woman was Zenobia." That part about hoping it was Zenobia just popped out of nowhere, or if I *had* hoped it, or even *thought* it, I wasn't aware of it until just then.

"C'mon," said Maddie, leading the way into the hall and looking up at the painting.

"Uh-uh," said Jill after a while. "Can't be our grandmother. *That* woman looks contented."

"Yes," I said. "Maybe that's why I hoped it was. And then last night, did you see how almost happy she looked when she was talking about our grandfather's work? Almost sort of glowing."

"Bizarre," said Jill.

"Yeah," said Maddie. "I mean paintings are *nice*, but they're

158

not *people*. What are you supposed to do when you want to see your family—go to a museum?"

I trailed along after my cousins, upstairs and down, while they chose paintings, then changed their minds, and chose others. When they had finally decided, we wrote it all down: what the pictures were of, and where they were hanging in the house. Then we took the list to our grandmother's room and handed it to her.

Zenobia read it and read it again. She folded it and tucked it into the front of her blouse and let out a long, slow "Hmmmmmph." Then she made you're-out-of-here motions with her hands.

Couldn't she say something? I thought. *Couldn't she even tell us about those particular pictures and why Lambert Jones painted them? Or when? Or . . .*

And right at that moment, I didn't care if I saw my grandmother or any of my grandfather's paintings ever again.

All the parents left on Sunday night, and an empty feeling settled over Fernhill. But if Sunday night seemed empty, then the rest of the week was even emptier. With a kind of finality to it.

Zenobia retreated to her room and more or less stayed there. Jill, Maddie, and I took turns going in one at a time, to try and spend time with her. But whenever we did, it was as if she had climbed into herself, and wasn't coming out, and pretty soon we gave up.

Maybe it was because of our grandmother's weird silence, but suddenly taking care of her seemed to be wearing her aides down. They were both really, really tired, I guess from working all those extra shifts, too. Audrey was looking forward to having some time off before her next job, and Ada told us about the trip to New England she was taking once Zenobia went to the Blackstone.

Even though our project to entertain Zenobia had come to a screeching halt, it somehow didn't seem right for us to head down to the shops, or even the library. So we mostly hung out on the front porch—and talked.

Not that we hadn't been talking all summer, but now we *really* talked. About anything. And everything. We talked about our parents and how they could sometimes be so incredibly embarrassing. We talked about boys, and teachers, and all the things we had ever wanted to be when we grew up but didn't want to be anymore. And what we *did* want to be. We each told one thing we had never revealed to another living soul, and got to ask one question apiece that another person *had* to answer.

"Do you like being half black?" was what Maddie asked me one afternoon while we were sitting on the porch putting polish on our toenails.

"I don't know—I never think about it," I said. "Except one time in second grade when a black kid called me an Oreo and a white kid called me a zebra all on the same day, and I went home and told my parents, and they said I am who I am and that's the only thing that matters. Why? Do you like being all white?"

"I don't know," said Maddie. "I never think about it."

And for some reason that struck us as incredibly funny, and we rolled around the porch floor, holding our stomachs and smearing our nail polish, so that once we caught our breath again we had to do our toes all over.

It rained all day Thursday. Late in the afternoon we were sitting in the living room, where we seemed to have been sitting all day, bored out of our minds and listening to Zenobia scream at Audrey.

"Do you think we really should worry?" asked Jill, flipping the TV on and then off again.

"About what?" I said. "Audrey can take care of herself."

"No, not that. About the fact that Zenobia is our grandmother and we have her genes. What happens if we got *the mean gene* and turn out just like her?" said Jill. "What if one of us starts acting that way? And starts wielding umbrellas and baseball bats?"

"None of us will," said Maddie, pushing herself out of her slouch so that she was sitting up straight.

Jill crinkled her forehead and said, "How can you be sure?"

"Because *we'll* be there, the other two of us, I mean," I said. "And we'll stop her. We'll remind her of the anti-Zenobia pact and tell her to cut it out—to shape up. No two ways about it."

"You're positive?" said Jill.

"Positively positive," said Maddie. "It's a promise."

"Let's shake on it," I said, sticking my feet out so that Maddie could pile hers on top of mine, and Jill put hers on top of both of ours in some weird this-is-forever pact.

The next day was Friday. The parents came back. And it was time for Zenobia to leave.

21

On Saturday afternoon my father and the uncles took the Morris chair, Zenobia's desk, the three paintings, and a clutter of boxes and bags and bundles over to the Blackstone. Mom and her sisters followed a little later to, as Aunt Claire put it, "get everything in proper order."

With the grownups gone and Michael and Steven in front of the TV watching an Orioles game, Jill, Maddie, and I wandered through the house as if we were taking part in the last scenes of a three-Kleenex movie. We went slowly, moving from floor to floor and room to room, touching the one-eyed rocking horse and the old dolls, the stuffed owl and the African masks. It was as if by touching all the things in the house we were somehow sealing them into memory.

Just as we were circling the downstairs hall for the second time, Zenobia came thumping out of her room, whacking at the doorframe and saying, "*Lackadaisical* is almost as bad as *slothful.* Can't you girls find any better way to occupy your time?" Then, without waiting for an answer, she thumped back the way she had come. And that was the last we saw of her until the next morning, when she was ready to leave.

Audrey and Ada took Zenobia to the Blackstone in Audrey's car. They also took the cat, Eleven, and were to drop him off with Mr. Rhea, the caretaker, on their way in.

"What happens if Zenobia doesn't like him—the cat man, I mean?" asked Jill.

"They'll turn around and come back, probably," said Maddie.

"And then we can start all over again," I added. And because with Zenobia we were never really sure about anything, we let a good two hours go by before we were able to breathe a sigh of relief.

With Zenobia gone, by midday Sunday the house was emptier than empty. We all crowded into the kitchen one last time and pieced together a let's-clean-everything-out-of-the-refrigerator lunch. Then Aunt Claire drew herself up tall and called out her final orders.

"You three girls get your things from the third floor. Michael and Steven, take out the trash. Elinor, Joyce, and I'll make sure everything is as it should be, and you men check the windows to see if they're shut, and stand by to lock the doors when we're all

163

out. Then we can head over to the Blackstone to make sure Zenobia's settled in—and still be on the way home before it's too late."

When we got to Zenobia's room, Audrey and Ada were still there, along with Mr. Prem and the nurse from the desk at the end of the hall. We stood there in an awkward silence until Uncle Ben and Aunt Claire and my mother started calling out introductions.

"Excuse me," snorted Zenobia, slapping a folded newspaper onto the arm of her chair. "This ragtag group is my family." And with that she used her cane to point us out, one by one, as she pronounced our names.

That turned out to be the highlight of the visit, and from then on, it was all downhill. There were little scraps of side conversations, some fidgeting, and a lot of jostling for seats (Michael and Steven). After what seemed like at least a day and a half Aunt Claire looked at her watch and said, "Well, Mother . . ."

"Well, Claire," said Zenobia matter-of-factly.

"We all have long drives ahead of us, so we should probably get on the road. But I'll run over next week . . ." Aunt Claire's words drifted off.

"We'll call," said Aunt Elinor, "and be back before you know it."

"It's hardly any distance by train," put in my mother.

Then suddenly we were in some hodgepodge of a line, moving forward to kiss Zenobia on her cool, wrinkled forehead.

And all the while, as I inched my way along, I kept sending her a message in my head. *Don't just let us go like this . . . Say something . . . say something . . . say something . . .*

Did she—or didn't she? I don't know, but there was some kind of choky noise in my grandmother's throat that could have been *Thank you* or *I liked meeting you* or *Come back soon.*

Did she—or didn't she? Yes or no? I'll never be sure—but I know what I think. I know what I think.

Epilogue

I was sixteen when I went back to Fernhill for my grandmother's funeral. Actually, it was a memorial service, planned in detail by Zenobia herself before she got too sick to care about things.

We were staying in a hotel downtown—Aunt Claire, Uncle Frank, Maddie and the twins, Aunt Elinor and Uncle Ben and Jill, my mom and dad and I—the way we always had when we'd come to Baltimore to see Zenobia in the last few years. Mostly we did those visits one family at a time, but even so, Maddie and Jill and I still had plenty of cousin time. At the beach in summer, or during the school year when we'd get together in New York, or Philadelphia, or Virginia.

As for our visits to the Blackstone—they were, well, they were disappointing. Zenobia never did turn into the grandmother that, despite my mother's warnings, I had hoped was hiding deep inside her. In fact, each time we saw her it was as if she'd inched further and further away, and the saddest part was when she stopped shaking her cane and fussing at us altogether. When she eventually stopped talking.

We all met at the hotel late on Friday afternoon, and once we were assembled, we went down to the harbor and caught the water taxi over to Fells Point for dinner. After we ate, we walked around the streets, people-watching and eating ice cream cones, and by the time we headed back it was dark and the lights of the harbor looked magical, and a little mysterious.

The next day, we just hung out until it was time to go to the memorial service and then all piled into our cars. Our fathers drove, one behind the other, like some mini funeral procession, out to Fernhill.

The house was crowded with people we didn't know, from the Art Institute, from New York and Washington, and even from California. Dr. Roloson, the head of the institute, greeted us on the porch and managed to find space for us in the back of the living room, and as soon as we were properly in place the service began.

Speeches. And more speeches. The really weird thing was that they were all about Lambert Jones, and not about Zenobia at all—except to say how she had been his "helpmate" and "supporter of his endeavors." Things like that.

I stood first on one foot and then the other, spacing out and watching a wasp trapped on the inside of the window. After I-don't-know-how-long, Maddie jabbed me in the ribs and I came back to earth in time to hear Dr. Roloson saying, ". . . iced tea and lemonade in the dining room and the garden . . . feel free to walk around . . ."

"C'mon," said Jill, and the three of us wormed our way through the crowd and into the hall. The paintings were gone, and the walls had been painted a clean, uncluttered cream. The clocks were still there, and the masks and the one-eyed rocking horse with the scraggly tail; the copper kettle, the sculptures, and the little chairs. But without paintings, it was as if the life had been drained out of the house.

"Upstairs," said Maddie. "Let's start at the top, with our room."

We made our way past expanses of bare cream walls to the third floor, where we found that the front room—our room—had been turned into a study area. There were tables and chairs, bookcases and file cabinets. Our beds were gone, and the movie posters; and the place where my mother had written THIS IS JOYCE'S SPACE was painted the color of a clay flowerpot, as was the rest of the room.

Without saying anything, we headed down, through the second floor and back to the hall, out the front door and around the side of the house. There was a woman standing there with some kind of badge on a string around her neck. "The studio is open," she said. "Lambert Jones's studio. If you girls would like to take a look."

We stepped inside, breathing the sharp, cool air and looking around. All of a sudden, I caught hold of Maddie with one hand, Jill with the other. "Look," I said. "Just look."

And there, on the side wall of our grandfather's studio, were the three paintings my cousins and I had chosen for Zenobia to take to the Blackstone.

"She must have left instructions for them to be hung here," said Jill.

"It looks—*right* somehow," said Maddie.

"Because they belong here," I whispered.

We stood there for a while and then began to move around the studio, reaching out but not touching the palettes, the easels, the tubes of paint.

"What was he like—this grandfather of ours?" I asked.

"Distant," said Maddie. "Faraway."

"Yeah," said Jill. "It was—I mean, there was Lambert and Zenobia—and then there were the rest of us."

I went to stand in front of the pictures again, pointing to "mine"—the woman walking on the beach. "You know something?" I said. "I think that really was Zenobia, and she knew Lambert was watching her and that one day he'd paint what he saw. And I think she was happy."

"On account of anything to do with him made her happy," said Jill.

"I hope," sighed Maddie.

After that we turned and went outside, past the woman with the badge on a string, and sat down at the old green picnic table. The one where we'd sat my first morning at Fernhill.

"It's not the same," said Jill. "Well, sort of, but not really."

Suddenly a black cat jumped up onto the table and stretched out, waiting to be scratched.

"Eleven?" I said. "It can't be, but . . ."

"His name *is* Eleven," the badge-woman called over to us from her place by the door. "Mrs. Jones took him with her when she went, but he wasn't happy and she had him sent back here. We have a live-in caretaker, so it works out just fine."

"Eleven," said Maddie. "It's really you."

For a while we sat there, the three of us scratching the cat, two pale hands and one like mocha latte.

"It was all right, wasn't it?" said Jill.

"Our Fernhill summer?" asked Maddie.

"Uh-huh," said Jill, nodding.

"Better than all right," I said. "It was unforgettable."